**She still couldn't s...
because he was foo...**

She made a point of cl...
on the steps. Finally th...

And Rory was suddenly glad that she had reached
the bottom of the steps or she might very well have
fallen over her feet.

Gage Stanton was gorgeous. Seriously, stupefyingly,
studly gorgeous.

Her mouth wanted to drool. Her brain wanted to get
him moving on his way as quickly as possible. She
was a thirty-three-year-old single mom who was
trying to keep the family business afloat.

She did *not* have time to be drooling over one of
the ranch guests, even if he were paying them an
exorbitant amount of money to learn their so-called
secrets of success.

She put on her usual greet-the-guests smile as she
closed the remaining distance between them.

"Welcome to the Angel River Ranch. I'm
Rory McAdams. I manage the property here. You
must be—"

"Gage Stanton," he said in a deep voice. The kind
of voice that made enticing shivers dance across a
woman's shoulders before slipping down her spine
to points beyond.

RETURN TO THE DOUBLE C:
Under the big blue Wyoming sky,
this family discovers true love!

Dear Reader,

One of the fun things about writing about families as extensive as the Clays and the Templetons is finally having a long-ago planned secret finally come to fruition in a story of its own.

That's the case with Gage Stanton and Rory McAdams. Gage has been hovering in the background for a while—in just my mind for even longer!—and it is such a pleasure to see him moving to the forefront. Not that it's an easy time for Gage. He has problems with his younger brother. He's an avowed workaholic. An avowed loner. But for all his reluctance to face his family secret, he has been slowly, steadily making steps in that direction whether he wants to admit it or not.

Falling for a single mom with a beautiful spirit and an enormous heart is just the push he needs to cross the finish line. Both with the family in the past he's never been a part of and the family of his future.

I hope you'll enjoy the journey.

Allison

Something About the Season

ALLISON LEIGH

HARLEQUIN

SPECIAL
EDITION

ISBN-13: 978-1-335-89489-2

Something About the Season

Copyright © 2020 by Allison Lee Johnson

All rights reserved. No part of this book may be used or reproduced in any manner whatsoever without written permission except in the case of brief quotations embodied in critical articles and reviews.

This is a work of fiction. Names, characters, places and incidents are either the product of the author's imagination or are used fictitiously. Any resemblance to actual persons, living or dead, businesses, companies, events or locales is entirely coincidental.

This edition published by arrangement with Harlequin Books S.A.

For questions and comments about the quality of this book, please contact us at CustomerService@Harlequin.com.

Harlequin Enterprises ULC
22 Adelaide St. West, 40th Floor
Toronto, Ontario M5H 4E3, Canada
www.Harlequin.com

Printed in U.S.A.

Though her name is frequently on bestseller lists, **Allison Leigh**'s high point as a writer is hearing from readers that they laughed, cried or lost sleep while reading her books. She credits her family with great patience for the time she's parked at her computer, and for blessing her with the kind of love she wants her readers to share with the characters living in the pages of her books. Contact her at allisonleigh.com.

Books by Allison Leigh

Harlequin Special Edition

Return to the Double C

A Weaver Christmas Gift
One Night in Weaver...
The BFF Bride
A Child Under His Tree
Yuletide Baby Bargain
Show Me a Hero
The Rancher's Christmas Promise
A Promise to Keep
Lawfully Unwed
Something About the Season

The Fortunes of Texas: The Lost Fortunes

Fortune's Texas Reunion

The Fortunes of Texas: Rambling Rose

The Texan's Baby Bombshell

Visit the Author Profile page
at Harlequin.com for more titles.

*For Greg, who can always make me laugh,
even when we're social distancing.*

Chapter One

"What fresh hell is this?"

Gage Stanton ignored his brother's question as they rolled to a stop in front of the entrance to Angel River Ranch. It had taken hours to reach what was just a tiny map dot near the Wyoming/Montana border.

Noah sat forward in his seat, raking his fingers through his hair as he surveyed the landscape beyond the windows of Gage's BMW. "This blows," he muttered, not for the first time since they'd left the courthouse in Denver that morning.

"Would you rather be sitting in jail for the next few months?"

Noah's lips thinned. He was twenty-two years old. Spoiled. Selfish.

Rich, except that Gage had managed to secure the bulk of Noah's inheritance so he couldn't squander it. Still, he consistently blew through his extremely generous allowance.

"I wouldn't be in jail," he muttered after Gage had rounded another curve. "Archer would have gotten me off."

"Kid, the only reason you're not in jail is because I convinced the judge that working for me would put you back on the straight and narrow." Not that Noah had *ever* walked the straight and narrow path. Before she'd died, it had been one of their mother's greatest regrets. "And Archer Templeton is my attorney. Not yours." He wouldn't admit how many times his lawyer had already intervened on his brother's behalf. But even Archer was fed up.

Noah drew himself up tight. "Don't call me *kid*."

"Then stop acting like one," Gage snapped. He turned onto the dirt road and drove through the guest ranch entrance marked by a forged iron sign.

He should have taken time to get an SUV. Something more suited to driving in this backwater than his M8.

Considering the rates Angel River commanded, he was surprised by the primitive road. He made a mental note to check about the roads getting in and out of the Rambling Rad Ranch.

He still wasn't sure what had prompted him to become the majority partner in the guest ranch development in the first place. He built luxury resorts.

Master planned communities. Industrial complexes. Not places where people went to pretend they were cowboys. And he didn't work with partners—even when they happened to be former employees that he trusted.

It wasn't that it was a *bad* plan. The Rad was located—literally—right on the edge of Rambling Mountain. The Wyoming mountain had, until earlier that year, been privately owned by an old man who'd never shared an acre of his property with anyone. Now, Otis Lambert was gone and Gage had won an expensive bidding war to purchase the decrepit cattle ranch. Because of Gage's new partnership with April Dalloway and her husband, Jed, the stakes to turn it into something successful were even higher. It wasn't only Gage's investment on the line. Aside from the expensive—but relatively simple—purchase of the ranch itself, use of the remainder of the mountain remained uncertain.

In his will, Otis Lambert had stipulated that the mountain beyond the ranch borders be for public use—ideally a state park—but so far nothing was set. As the matter languished on the vine because of politics and budget constraints, Archer had been bugging Gage to get involved at the local level—namely the town of Weaver, located closest to the mountain. Because if the land didn't become a state park, it would fall under Weaver control. But Gage preferred keeping his distance from Weaver for reasons that had nothing to do with getting into the guest ranch business or who ended up in control of the pristine mountain wilderness that surrounded it.

Gage had always believed that good business trumped personal business. It's what had gotten him this far in life. But in this case, Weaver was way too close to personal.

"Doesn't look like much." Noah's morose voice brought Gage's thoughts back to the present.

He had to agree. The curving road bisected one side of nothing and the other side of nothing. There were no trees to speak of. There wasn't anything particularly green. The fields had bypassed gold and headed straight into brown.

He couldn't blame that on anything other than the time of year, though. It was the end of October. Back home in Denver, it had already snowed once that month before temperatures soared back up again. When he'd spoken with Sean McAdams, the owner at Angel River, Sean had told him they probably wouldn't see snow until after Thanksgiving. But Gage should pack for it. Just in case.

Since he hadn't really planned to make this jaunt to Nowhere, Wyoming, in the first place, he hadn't put a lot of advance thought into what he'd thrown into his suitcase. He traveled a lot. He'd grabbed the usual stuff and pitched it in.

His lawyer had told him about the Angel River property a few months ago. It had plenty of travel and leisure awards to its credit and was one of the most well-regarded guest ranches in the Western United

States. Based on Archer's research, Gage had arranged to send Wade Jenkins from his office to find out what did and didn't work for Angel River. Gage had been ready to pay the price for that research, too. Not just the cost of lodging Wade for a couple weeks, but compensation to Angel River for behind-the-scenes information that would be used by the Rad, which—in time—would be their competitor. Sean had agreed to the plan.

Then the situation with Noah had reared its ugly head.

Gage damn sure hadn't planned on coming here himself, much less with his spoiled half brother in tow. But during court that morning he'd felt forced to act.

Because before she died, Gage had made an impossible promise to his mother that he'd always watch out for him.

Noah's latest stunt to land him in front of a judge again had been crashing his car through the plate-glass window of a Denver high-rise. A high-rise that Gage owned.

Thankfully, Noah hadn't hurt anyone. Not even himself.

Of course, he'd been drunk, despite just spending weeks in a rehab facility.

He'd also been pissed at Gage for finally telling him his allowance was being cut off. For telling him that he needed to find a job. Go to work and be a productive member of society.

Needless to say, Noah hadn't been happy. He was the only heir of a pharmaceutical magnate. He didn't "do" work.

Gage's choice that morning had been to either let his brother see serious jail time for this latest escapade or personally guarantee that Noah would stay sober and productive.

He'd called the owner of Angel River yet again with a change in plans. Squirreling Noah away at the ranch for a month and a half would either be Gage's best idea ever or one of his very worst.

He squelched a sigh and continued following the dirt road until it took a sharp turn. Suddenly they were overlooking a verdant strip of land. Autumn-hued trees clung to the banks of a glittering river that flowed past a large lodge situated on a hill. Several other smaller buildings were scattered on both sides of the river.

Horses grazed in a pen some distance away from the lodge, and even farther beyond that, Gage could see cattle milling around and a few figures on horseback. It looked as picture-perfect as it did on the ranch's slick website.

"What am I supposed to be doing here, anyway?" Noah's sulky tone raked on Gage's patience.

He pulled up to a glorified shack bearing a stop-here sign. "It's a ranch," he said flatly. "I'm pretty sure there'll be plenty of things to keep you busy."

Noah started muttering what he thought about that, but he broke off and rolled down his window when the young woman who'd stepped out of the shack approached his side of the car.

She leaned down to look through the window, wearing a smile that spread all the way to her sparkling eyes. "Welcome to Angel River. You must be Mr. Stanton."

"*He* is," Noah said with a jerk of his head.

Despite Noah's sullen tone, her smile didn't waver. "I'm Marni. If you'll pull up to the main lodge, they've been expecting you." She gestured toward the log building situated on the knoll, her bright gaze skipping from Gage's face to Noah's and then back again. "You'll have a chance to settle in, but don't take too long. Everyone's already gathering at the barn for the afternoon activity. Here's a map of the property." She thrust a black-and-white brochure through the window at Noah then stepped back from the car. "Enjoy your stay!"

Gage watched her practically skip back toward the shed, her spiky pink hair bouncing. "Cute."

Noah just made a grunting sound. If he appreciated the girl's cheerful friendliness or gamine prettiness, he obviously wasn't going to say.

Gage was damned if he knew what qualities actually interested Noah. He'd never seemed to date a girl more than a few times.

But then, the same thing could be said about himself. He'd been married once. Briefly and a long time ago. As exes, he and Jane were a lot happier with each other than they'd ever been when they'd been married. Now she was married to a decent guy who gave her the sort of time a man should give his wife. Should *want* to give his wife. They even had kids.

But Gage had learned his lesson. He liked playing to his strengths. Relationships weren't one of them.

He continued on to the lodge while Noah looked at the map.

The closer they got, the more rutted the road became. By the time Gage parked between a couple of muddy vehicles, he'd decided that *all* the access roads to the Rad would be paved. Just because the place wouldn't be one of his typical luxury resorts, guests still shouldn't have to worry about taking out an axel before they even reached their destination.

As Noah just sat there, Gage climbed out of the car with relief and pulled out his cell phone. There was barely any signal. Regardless of the reasons that had brought him here, Gage still had a business to run. He hoped the ranch at least had decent Wi-Fi.

"Come on," he told his brother. "Sitting there sulking isn't going to change anything."

From inside the vehicle, Noah told Gage what he could go and do with himself.

Gage almost smiled.

His brother was nothing if not consistent.

Inside the lodge's office, Rory McAdams stood at the window and watched the tall man climb from his low-slung black vehicle. He was too far away to see his face, but everything about him looked impatient.

From the fingers he thrust through his dark hair to the way he looked at his cell phone and wristwatch.

On top of everything else, he was going to be one of *those*.

The kind of guest who arrived all tensed up and would stay that way once he realized that all of his fancy little tech devices didn't count for squat here. The ranch provided wireless internet, but it wasn't exactly the lightning-fast variety. The phones were connected by that old-fashioned thing called wire. There weren't even televisions inside the guest rooms, and the newspaper that her father still insisted on subscribing to was always delivered several days late.

She glanced over her shoulder at him. Despite the latest tests that said Sean McAdams's cancer hadn't returned after two years, the battle had left its mark. He looked a fraction of the man who had been at the helm of Angel River for nearly all of her life.

"He's here," she said.

Her father nodded. "I told you he would come." He gave her a pointed look that was reminiscent of his precancer days. "No matter how much you hoped he wouldn't."

Rory swallowed the denial on the tip of her tongue. What her father said was true.

"Better go and greet him," her dad prompted. "He's a paying guest."

"Gage Stanton's a competitor," she muttered. One who wanted to pick their brains for every secret to their success just so he could turn around and use that information against them.

Aware of the way her dad was watching her, she tightened the ponytail at the back of her head, picked up two of the gift bags they always presented to incoming guests and left the office. Maybe her steps were a little more like stomps, but she couldn't help it.

Aside from the arrangement he'd made with Stanton, her dad hadn't made a single decision where the ranch was concerned since he'd gotten sick. What other things might he be planning without telling her?

The office had once been on the third floor with windows that afforded its occupants a near-panoramic view of the main ranch. Since her dad's health had declined, they'd relocated it to the main floor, taking over a guest suite. It was convenient for him since there was a fully equipped bedroom. It meant he could rest whenever he'd needed to without returning to his cabin located a few miles away.

Now that he was feeling better, they could have moved the office back to its original location, freeing up the room for bookings again.

Only there'd been no need.

Right now, the lodge was quiet, but its peacefulness didn't soothe her like it usually did.

The lunch hour had passed. Bart had cleared everything away, and the guests were off on their afternoon activities. Frannie, she hoped, was cleaning the guest rooms while they were empty.

Rory reached the lodge entrance and pushed her lips into a smile she didn't feel before pulling open the heavy door. The wind whipped at her ponytail as she stepped outside. She gathered it over one shoulder, trying to keep it under control as she walked along the wide porch toward a set of stairs that led down to the driveway.

Most guests preferred to fly. Wymon, the nearest town, had an airstrip the ranch paid to maintain just so their guests would have an easier time reaching them. The fact that Stanton had chosen to drive such an impractical vehicle here only underscored the fact that he wasn't a typical guest.

She still couldn't see the man's face. He was too busy with his cell phone.

This time she deliberately clomped her boots just to get his attention. Finally he lifted his head and looked her way.

Rory was immediately glad that she'd already reached the bottom of the steps, or she might have fallen over her feet.

Gage Stanton—assuming the new arrival *was* Gage Stanton and not the other guest he'd told her dad he was bringing—was gorgeous. Seriously, studly gorgeous.

So gorgeous that it was an effort to get her mouth to work in conjunction with her brain. Her mouth wanted to drool. Her brain wanted to get him moving on his way as quickly as possible. She was a thirty-three-year-old single mom trying to keep the family business afloat and did *not* have time to be drooling over anyone. Least of all someone who'd paid them a fortune to learn their so-called secrets of success.

The last time she'd drooled over someone, she'd ended up with Killian. And though she wouldn't trade her son for the world—he *was* her world after all—she wasn't prepared for a repeat.

Not that the gorgeous black-haired man looking back at her with meltingly beautiful brown eyes would ever drool over *her*.

Undoubtedly, his last-minute guest was one of the female variety. He wouldn't be the first of her guests with "companions" they preferred to keep discreet.

If they paid their fees and didn't cause any damage to the property or her staff, who was Rory to judge?

Anyway, she never got involved with guests. Not that way. Especially guests who brokered deals with her father behind her back.

As she closed the distance between them, she made an effort to put on her usual greet-the-guests smile. "Good afternoon. Welcome to the Angel River Ranch." She extended one of the tote bags fashioned with the ranch's logo of unfurled wings superimposed over a curving river. "I'm Rory Mc-Adams. I manage the property here. You must be—"

"Gage Stanton," he said in a deep voice. The kind

of voice that made shivers dance across a woman's shoulders before slipping down her spine to points beyond.

Her practiced smile didn't waver. "I'm glad you made it safely. Much longer and we would have been sending out a search party for you." She wasn't joking, though she said it lightly.

His perfectly molded lips tilted slightly. "Sorry about that." He lifted his phone. "Would have called to let you know we'd be arriving later than planned, but—" A faint line appeared in his lean cheek as his smile deepened. "I keep forgetting that there are still places in the world where these barely work."

The self-deprecating smile was almost enough to throw her.

Almost.

"You're here now, so that's what counts." She looked toward the car. The front window was almost as heavily tinted as the side windows, and she could barely make out a slender figure with dark hair in the passenger seat. "Now let's get you settled so you both can begin enjoying your stay."

The developer opened his door and angled his head to look in at his companion. "Get moving." His voice was short to the point of rude before he shut the door again with a decisive click.

Oh. Kay. Then.

She would be discreet about this guest if it choked her, but it would be even harder if the guy turned out to be a total jerk. No matter *how* much money he was paying them. On the other hand, if he *was* a jerk, he could learn all of Angel River's secrets and he'd still fail, because nobody liked visiting a guest ranch that was being run by a jerk.

As if it were a weather vane, she felt her sympathy suddenly swing around in the direction of the man's companion.

Stanton stepped forward and took the tote bag from her. His fingers barely grazed hers as he took the strap, but it was enough to make her shiver yet again.

Dang it all.

She deliberately moved away from him and crossed to the other side of the luxurious car.

"Good afternoon," she said brightly as she pulled open the door for the poor woman inside. "Welcome to Angel River."

But it wasn't a woman who uncoiled herself from the seat.

It was a man.

Young.

Painfully thin.

He was almost as handsome as Gage, but in a less-finished way. And his face also had a distinctive pallor that reminded her of her father's.

She felt her practiced smile soften, feeling even more sympathy. Man. Woman. What did it matter? Suffering was suffering.

"I'm Rory." She extended her hand to him. "If

there is anything I can do to make your stay here more enjoyable, all you have to do is say the word."

He suddenly smiled. His eyes were blue. Set off by all that dark hair and stubbled jaw, they were quite striking. "Word," he said and clasped her hand.

His fingers were cool. They did *not* send shivers down her spine.

"Give the woman back her hand, Noah." Gage had moved around to open the trunk and was lifting out a small suitcase that looked brand-new and a second bag that looked anything but. "You'll have to excuse my brother, Rory." He pushed the trunk closed. "He obviously doesn't know how to behave around a pretty woman."

Chapter Two

*B*rother?

Pretty?

Rory wasn't sure which word surprised her more.

There was no way he meant the "pretty" thing. She was under no delusions when it came to her own looks. Thirty-three-year-old single mothers like her had more pressing things to do with their time than regularly sit themselves down in a chair at the beauty salon. Her hair needed a good five-inch trim, and she couldn't remember the last time she'd filed—much less polished—her fingernails.

Stanton probably tossed that phrase around whenever he was in the vicinity of a woman.

Her friend Megan would've objected that his words were hardly politically correct in this day and age and that Rory was a ninny for not pointing it out to him.

Fortunately, Megan, who was also the ranch's head wrangler, wasn't here. So Rory, whether she believed Gage or not, could secretly enjoy hearing the word *pretty* being applied to her.

Particularly since his unnamed guest turned out to be his *brother, not a mistress*.

Maybe she was getting cynical. Painting guests with too broad a brush.

She ignored the fact that her step felt springier as she began walking them to their lodgings. She had a job to do—get them settled—and a limited amount of time in which to do it because of their late arrival.

She gestured to the cabins situated on the other side of the gravel road. "We had the original reservation assigned to a room in the lodge. But considering how long you're planning to stay, I've moved you instead to the Brown cabin. As you can see, it's almost as close to the river as the lodge. You'll have more privacy and space. But if you prefer more interaction with other guests, I can move you back to a room in the lodge."

"Rooms," Gage and Noah both said at the same time.

She glanced at them. The two seemed to be making a point of not looking at each other.

Aside from the espresso-dark hair the two men shared, Rory didn't see much of a physical resemblance between them. When it came to surveying everything around them as they crossed the road, though, the expressions on their faces could have belonged to twins.

Neither one looked enthusiastic about being there. Which made her wonder why Gage had not only taken the place of his employee and lengthened the original reservation, but brought Noah along as well.

They reached the cabin and she unlocked the door, dropped the key into Gage's palm without any contact and led the way inside.

She turned to watch them enter, gauging their reaction. The two-story, two-bedroom unit was spotless and had been carefully maintained. However, the Western-style furnishings were more than a decade old and in her opinion could stand some updating.

If it weren't for her father's medical bills, she'd have worked some needed renovations into the budget by now.

"The kitchen is stocked, but you're welcome to join us for meals. Breakfast is always in the breakfast room, but the location for lunch and dinner can change from day to day. You'll find a brochure with menus, locations and times in your welcome totes. As you know, we're all-inclusive here. No hidden fees are going to be sprung on you. It's entirely up to you how much or how little you want to do while you're here, and that includes satisfying your appetites. In terms of activities, all you have to do is show up at the activity barn on time. Every outing begins there." She glanced at her watch. "It's too late to participate in one this afternoon, but since you missed the lunch hour, I can get something prepared for you both."

"That won't be—" Gage started to say.

"That sounds great," Noah said over him.

She hesitated, looking from one to the other.

Gage dropped the suitcase and the battered bag on the floor inside the door. His dark brown gaze slid from his brother to her. "Guess we'll take you up on that, Rory."

Shivers again.

Darn it.

It was safer focusing on his right ear than getting trapped in his deep brown gaze. "I'll let you settle in, then," she said. "Head on back up to the lodge whenever you're ready. If I'm not there, Chef Bart will take good care of you."

Without waiting for a response, she hurried out the door, pulling it closed behind her.

Gravel scraped under her boots as she crossed the road that wove between the cabins and the lodge before branching out toward the activity barn in one direction and the river in the other.

Typically at this time of year—when the autumn colors were on full display and the weather still allowed for lots of outdoor activities—all of their units would be occupied. That included the ones here in the main camp as well as those near Angel's Lookout. Even the Uptown Camp didn't go more than a week without a booking. Maybe there'd be a room or two open in the lodge, but never had they had more vacancies than occupancies.

Except this year.

It was an unpalatable truth that the fees Gage Stanton had paid—in advance, no less—were more welcome than ever.

She glanced at her watch again as she entered the lodge. The school bus would be arriving soon, and she quickened her step through the soaring great room, then the breakfast room and finally into the kitchen. Their chef, Bartholomew Lavigne—or Chef Bart, since he'd decided a long time ago that the moniker was more fitting for a Western guest ranch—was sitting on a stool at the stainless steel counter with a big calendar in front of him. She knew from experience that he was working out the menus for November. Typically, that would include a special Thanksgiving week, but she wasn't even sure yet how many guests they'd have by the holiday week.

She'd even been considering closing the property—unheard-of in Angel River's history—for that week until her father had told her about Gage Stanton suddenly extending his stay.

"The Brown cabin party arrived," she told Bart.

"Another guy bringing a woman who's not his wife?"

His dry humor brightened her spirits. "I don't know where you get such a suspicious mind. Two brothers," she said. "Gage and Noah. Do you mind putting together some lunch for them?"

Bart gave her a look above the rims of his black-framed glasses. "And if I do?"

She smiled. "You'll do it anyway, because you always do what's necessary. That's why I love you."

"That's what all the pretty girls say."

There was that word again.

But she'd been hearing it from Bart, who was a very spry sixty-five, since she'd been a child.

"I'm going down to meet the bus, but when I get back we can go over your calendar."

"You've decided what to do about Thanksgiving week, then?"

"The week is going to occur whether we have more bookings or not," she said with more spirit than she felt. "It certainly won't be as busy as the week before, what with the Pith wedding." That had been a huge booking, made just that summer and worth almost as much as the "consulting" fee that Stanton had paid them. "Just plan for everything like usual for now."

Bart's gaze was steady over his horn-rims. "You're sure?"

Despite her misgivings, she nodded. "I don't think holding off another week will make a difference," she admitted. "At least if we finalize everything now, I'll have plenty of time to print up the menus and schedules well before we get busy with the wedding group." She'd taken over that particular task since they'd lost their office assistant the year before. It wasn't everyone's cup of tea to live and work on a remote guest ranch, and so far, finding someone to replace Kaisley had been a bust. The only bright spot had been saving the expense of her salary.

"Speaking of." He riffled through a folder and pulled out a stapled sheaf of order forms. "You owe me ten bucks." He waved the papers. "They chose a tiered cake over cupcakes. Four tiers."

"Four!" She made a face as she pulled a ten-dollar bill from her pocket and handed it over. "That's a lot of cake for thirty-six people."

"Small tiers," he allowed. "But I'm looking forward to something different. Been a while since we've had a traditional cake. Everybody's been having cupcakes or pie buffets and such."

"I'm happy for you," she said dryly as she headed for the rear entrance via the oversize storeroom. "I wish the other details of the wedding day were decided. Mrs. Pith keeps waffling over which location to use for the ceremony itself."

"I hid away a couple of muffins for Killy." Bart's voice followed her. "Send him in here when you get back."

"Will do!"

She took one of the UTVs parked in back of the lodge and was soon bumping her way along the gravel road. It was a mile and a half to the junction where the bus would stop. Plenty of time for the worries on her mind to whip back up again.

She could afford not to replace Kaisley just yet. But she couldn't afford not to replace the spa manager who'd quit three months ago, leaving only Donna, the part-timer, to bear that load. Unfortunately, Rory had been no more successful in finding a new manager than she'd been in finding a replacement for Kaisley. She also needed to either promote Frannie to head of housekeeping and give her the raise she'd been asking for or chance the longtime employee quitting if Rory hired someone else for the job.

She didn't want Frannie to leave. But she also didn't think she was entirely qualified for more responsibility. Things tended to fall through the cracks where Frannie was concerned, which meant the rest of the crew was often left picking up the slack.

Why couldn't Gage Stanton have come to learn the secrets of their success when Rory's father had been at the helm? At least then there wouldn't have been anything *but* success for him to learn.

And she wouldn't be worried that her dad was making secret deals with a developer known to take over struggling properties.

She reached the bus stop to find two other vehicles already there waiting. She waved to them as she parked in her usual spot. The dusty pickup truck belonged to Seth Riggs—there to pick up his daughter, Toonie. Seth ran the cattle operation. The herd wasn't merely for the purpose of lending the ranch authenticity. For as long as Rory could remember, it had been a minor moneymaker for Angel River.

Unless their season improved, that was not going to be the case this year.

Frannie's daughter, Astrid, was sitting behind the wheel of a UTV similar to Rory's, her head bouncing in time to the music only she could hear through her headphones. She was there to pick up her little brother, Damon, who was a year older than Killy and his best friend in the world.

To some, it might seem more logical for all of the schoolkids to be picked up by just one person from Angel River and delivered accordingly to their appropriate locations. But Seth lived nearly five miles away to the west, Frannie and her kids lived nearly three to the east, and Rory and Killian lived in a cabin two miles due north.

She heard the engine, chugging and wheezing, long minutes before the yellow nose of the bus appeared. Sound carried here in the valley. Sometimes when the wind was right, they could even hear semis from the highway.

She had to fight the urge to go over and meet Killy the second he got off the bus. That had been okay *last* year, when he'd been a "baby kindygarder"— his words. Now, though, he was in first grade. He didn't need his mommy waiting for him the moment he bounded out of the bus.

The day she'd learned *that*, she'd wanted to howl with tears.

The three kids from Angel River weren't the only ones still on the bus. It would continue on after this stop for another ten miles, where it would let off the remaining children. Then it would travel all the way back to Wymon. And in the early morning, it would repeat the route.

She couldn't remember how old she'd been when she'd started yearning for something more interesting than this corner of the world. When she'd wanted something more than Angel River. More than the same people day in and day out.

She'd learned the error of her ways, but she dreaded the day when Killy would begin to feel the same way. He'd want to go out and explore the world and she was going to be brokenhearted when he did.

Damon came off the bus first, followed by Killy soon after. Her heart squeezed at the sight of him. He was growing so much. Her baby boy was becoming a little man.

She waved at him. Unnecessarily, of course. None of the kids could fail to miss the presence of their rides.

He and Damon were tossing a football back and forth, and Rory bit the inside of her cheek to keep from smiling too broadly at the way her little boy struggled mightily to keep the football from falling through his arms.

Astrid yelled for Damon, and even from a distance, she could see the boys make faces at each other.

Killy threw the football in a wobbling arc back to Damon, nearly hitting Toonie as she hunched her way over to her dad's pickup. The young teenager had her nose buried in the book she carried. As usual.

Then Killy ran to the UTV and heaved his backpack in before clambering onto the seat next to her. "Damon got detention," he greeted breathlessly. "'Cause old man Frisk thought he threw a spitball at him."

"*Mr.* Frisk," Rory corrected as she started up the utility vehicle, even though Horace Frisk had been old when *she'd* had him in school. She sketched a wave toward Astrid and Seth as they all pulled out and drove away from the bus stop. Only once they'd left would the bus have room to turn around on the narrow road and head along its way. "And did Damon throw a spitball at him?"

"Nah." Killy shook his head, and his messy brown hair fell over his eyes. "It was Amy Carpenter, but Damon says he's gonna marry Amy so he hadda take the fall for her. 'Cause it's shovelruss."

She was used to deciphering, but that one took her a moment. "Chivalrous?"

"Uh-huh." He was leaning over to rummage inside his backpack. He pulled out a crumpled piece of paper. "Can we go to the Halloween carnival?"

He thrust the flyer practically in her face, and she caught it from him.

"I've told you before. We'll see."

His shoulders slumped. "That means no."

She tucked the sheet of paper under her thigh where it wouldn't blow away. "No, it doesn't." She turned onto the Angel River Loop that would carry them back toward the lodge and slowed almost to a crawl. "Give me a kiss."

Out of sight of his buddy, her little boy gave her a quick peck that was followed with a gratifyingly tight hug.

She squeezed him back, hanging on for a second longer just because he allowed it before he started squirming again and she had to let him go. "So what kind of day did *you* have at school?"

"I got a hundred on my spelling test."

"Good job!" She held up her palm, and he slapped his against it. "I told you that you could do it." When it came to math, her boy was off the charts. But spelling and English were another matter.

"Then can we go to the Halloween carnival?"

She gave him a sideways look. "When did you start thinking that earning good grades was a bargaining chip?"

He wrinkled his freckled nose at her. "What?"

She ruffled his hair. She really needed to get him in for a haircut. Usually they could do that sort of thing at the Angel Spa, but Donna was too busy on her own with the guests they *did* have. Maybe Rory could get him in somewhere in town after the carnival. Because there was very little likelihood that she wouldn't take him.

But she didn't want to be a pushover, either. "We can go to the Halloween carnival on Saturday *if* you do all of your chores for the rest of the week without fussing about them."

His dark blue eyes turned very serious as he thought about that. But then he shrugged, evidently deciding the carnival was worth that particular trouble for the next two days. "Okay. I'm hungry."

She smiled, her heart feeling full. Who needed anything else in the world as long as her little boy was around? She sped up again, stirring a cloud of dust behind them. "Fortunately, Chef Bart has you taken care of as usual. He has a muffin or two with your name on them."

"I like Chef Bart's muffins. They're way better'n yours," he said artlessly.

She laughed. "That's true, but it's not very polite telling me so." She could never hope to compete with Bart's kitchen skills. "What if you hurt my feelings?"

He gave her an alarmed look. "I didn't, though, did I?"

She gave him a wink. "Nope. But remember there are things you can say to me, 'cause I'm your mom and you can always tell me anything, and there are things you shouldn't say to people who aren't your mom."

"Like the lady who's with Mr. Pantano this time? She's not as pretty as the one he brought last time. I told Grandpa."

"Yes, like her," she said wryly. And wished that her son wasn't quite so observant about the guests. Generally, he didn't have a lot of interaction with them. He had school and homework during the week, and on Saturdays, he and Damon were usually involved in the sport of the month.

She decided to change the subject.

"So, *if* you do all your chores for the rest of the week without complaint and get to go to the carnival, what costume do you want to wear?" The days of kids wearing costumes to school had gone by the wayside, but she was glad to know that it was still encouraged for the carnival.

"Cap'n 'Merica," he said immediately. "Damon is, too, but we decided we could both be the same."

"That works out well, then." She followed the loop around to the east, heading back to the lodge. It also worked out well since Killy already had the basic elements of the costume. She could just spiff up the cardboard shield she'd already made for him last year. "Do you have any homework?"

He made a glum face. "Three whole worksheets."

"Maybe your grandpa can help you with them." Her dad had helped him achieve that perfect score on his spelling test after all. She pulled up behind the lodge and parked the UTV. "Go on in and see

Chef Bart for your snack," she told Killy. "I'll take care of your backpack."

He needed no further encouragement as he vaulted from the seat almost before the wheels had stopped. She heard the slam of the door cutting off his yelled "Hey, Chef Bart, I got an A-plus on my spelling—" before she'd even hefted his backpack over her shoulder.

Smiling to herself, she followed after him more slowly, reading the carnival flyer as she went. They weren't charging for the games like they had in the past but instead were asking for contributions of school supplies as the cost of admission. They provided a helpful list of items and the quantities needed.

She went through the storeroom, wondering how difficult it was going to be getting her hands on a half dozen wide-ruled notebooks or classroom-size bottles of hand sanitizer. It wasn't as if they had a Shop-World around the corner. With more notice, she could have ordered something online, but at this point there was no way anything would arrive before the weekend.

She entered the kitchen, shaking her head as she looked at the list. "Don't they realize it would be easier to charge admission and just have the schools buy what they need?" She waved the list in her hand and looked up, expecting to see Bart and Killy sitting at the counter in the kitchen.

They were nowhere in sight, however.

Instead, Gage Stanton was sitting at the stainless steel counter, once again with his phone in his hand. He had a plate next to his elbow. He'd eaten part of his hamburger and some of the sweet potato fries.

He raised a brow when she practically skidded to a halt. "I'll take a guess that you didn't mean that question for me."

She made a point of folding the flyer. "Elementary school stuff," she said and tucked the flyer in her back pocket. She told herself it was her imagination that his gaze seemed to follow her hand.

She pulled open the oversize refrigerator and extracted a small bottle of cranberry juice, then nudged the door closed with her hip. She pretended to focus on opening the bottle. "Did you see a small boy run through here?"

"About this tall?" He held out his palm. "Blue eyes like yours, plus freckles?"

Just because he noticed the color of her eyes was no reason to get sidetracked. "That'd be him."

Gage jerked his head toward the doorway. "Went that way with your chef."

"Thanks." She started to leave the room, but her conscience as a host made her hesitate. His water glass was nearly empty, and she picked up the pitcher nearby. "How is everything with your lunch? Is there anything you need?" She refilled his glass and grabbed the basket of cookies and chunky brownies that was usually kept in the breakfast room for guests to help themselves throughout the day.

She was surprised he hadn't chosen to sit there. The breakfast room had a beautiful view of the river.

She set the basket closer to him. "Something sweet? Chef Bart's triple-chocolate brownies are my personal downfall."

He didn't even glance at the basket, but the corner of his lips lifted slightly. "I'll have to remember that."

Warmth suffused her, and she set the pitcher down with what felt like glaring clumsiness. Considering it had been his brother who'd indicated interest in a meal earlier, she wondered why Gage was solo. "And your brother? Noah, he's—"

His dark, intense gaze finally released her when he looked at his phone once more. "He's fine."

She didn't like feeling dismissed.

But she also didn't want to hang around there any longer than necessary.

If he were any other guest—a regular guest—she would take the cue and leave him to his privacy. But he was not their typical guest. He was paying them an astronomical amount of money to learn how they operated. And even though it was her father with whom that bargain had been struck, it fell to Rory to see it through. "When would you like to, ah, to start—" She had trouble finding the adequate words.

He wasn't similarly afflicted. "Learning the ropes?"

She nodded, her lips pressed together in a smile that she hoped wasn't as stiff as it felt. "Once I get

Killy settled, I'll have some free time before the other guests begin returning from their afternoon activities, or…or maybe you'd like to just be a guest for a week?" She couldn't help feeling hopeful at the idea. "See things from that perspective first?"

He quickly dashed her hopes. "Your guest reviews are remarkably positive. So I think we can skip just being a guest. How about we start tomorrow morning?" His tone was smooth. "Let me know what your schedule is, and I'll just—" his gaze slid over her very briefly "—shadow you."

The skin over her spine tingled. She resolutely ignored it and trained her gaze squarely on his earlobe. "I'll put a schedule together for you by dinner."

"Perfect." He looked back at his phone. "Your chef got me onto your Wi-Fi. It's slow as hell."

"Yes, it is," she agreed matter-of-factly and left.

She tracked down her son and their chef in the office. Killy was covered in muffin crumbs while he regaled his grandfather with the day's spitball excitement.

She dropped Killy's backpack on the couch next to where he was sprawled. "Don't get too comfortable there, mister. You have worksheets to do, remember?"

He started rummaging in the depths of the backpack, coming out with the usual six-year-old boy detritus—some rocks, an unwrapped hard candy covered in lint, two plastic dinosaurs—before he pulled out a bundle of crumpled pages stapled together in one corner. "I got this, too." He handed it to her before diving back into the pack.

She took the packet, half-afraid to see what it was about. The last time he'd come home with a packet, it had been a recommendation for placing him in the gifted program because of his math skills.

But that would mean going to a school even farther away. Despite her reservations, she'd talked at length with his teacher and decided to put it off another year. This time, though, it was just registration information for the following school year. Nearly ten months away.

She decided the packet could wait and tossed it aside on her desk. Her father was already reviewing Killy's worksheets with him, and she glanced at the chef. "Do you want to go over your calendar now?"

Bart pushed himself up from his chair and, with a wrinkle of his nose, made his glasses that were propped against his forehead drop neatly down into place where they belonged. "I'll have biscotti for you after school tomorrow, buddy."

Killy grinned up at him. "I like biscotti."

The chef laughed. "You like everything, Killy. That's why you're growing like a weed."

Her little boy suddenly stood on the couch and shot his hand up in the air as high as it could reach. "I'm gonna be *this* tall. Like my dad."

Rory's gaze caught on her father's. Killy had mentioned his dad more than once lately. "Don't stand on the couch," she reminded him and headed out of the office along with Bart.

"How does he know—"

"He doesn't," Rory said before Bart could finish his question. Killian had never even met his father. Rory didn't have any pictures left of Jon, who had, indeed, been very tall. When he'd decided she and their future child weren't worth sticking around for, she'd decided photographs of him had to go, too. One of these days, she knew she was going to have to explain his absence to Killy, but for now she preferred to act as if the man had never existed.

A few of the other guests had returned to the lodge when Rory and Bart walked back through the great room, and she stopped off long enough to greet them.

Tig Pantano was a big bear of a man, handsome enough in his middle-aged way. He owned some sort of business in Colorado and was a regular guest at the ranch—usually staying a month at a time. The flavor of the month on his arm was a giggly, overly made-up blonde named Willow with the voice of a chipmunk who seemed to feel the need to gush over every blade of grass as if she'd never seen one before.

Maybe that's what she thought would impress Tig, and for all Rory knew, maybe it did. So far, she hadn't seen any similarities among Tig's companions except that they were female and none of them were actually his wife, Monica.

Rory had met her only once, several years earlier, when she and Tig had first visited the ranch. Since then, Rory spoke on the phone with Monica at least six times a year—every time she made a fresh reservation for her husband and his latest paramour. Monica even provided their names on the reservations.

It really did take all kinds.

Noah suddenly walked into the great room, and Willow abruptly broke off her latest bubbling rave over her afternoon boating trip. Her eyes followed the young man almost hungrily, and Rory felt an unexpected spurt of sympathy for Tig.

Fortunately, four more guests came in on Noah's heels, and the room livened up. Tig told Willow to put on some music while he headed behind the mahogany bar.

Noah was hovering around looking alone, and Rory went over to him. "Looking for your brother?"

"Surprised he's not looking for me," he muttered. "Since he's my new warden. And he's only my half brother."

He made it sound as if that mattered. Half or whole, it all counted in her book. But she wasn't sure what response was appropriate after the "warden" comment, so she gestured at the small crowd making themselves comfortable in the expansive great room. "Have you had a chance to look around yet? Meet any of the other guests?"

He shook his head.

There was still plenty of time to look over Bart's calendar. Particularly when her only part in the affair was to sign off on the supply order. "Well, then, how about I introduce you to everyone?" She became aware of Gage entering the room. Not only because of the fine prickling on the nape of her neck, but because of the tight expression on Noah's face.

For once, Gage's ever-present cell phone wasn't in his hand, and he'd obviously overheard her words. "You can introduce all of us," he said as he stopped next to her.

She felt that damnable shiver again.

Then she smiled weakly and began making introductions.

Chapter Three

There was a sharp nip in the air the next morning when Rory drove her UTV back to the ranch after seeing Killy onto the school bus.

It was early yet, and even though she could have driven back up to the house to spend another hour in the haven of her warm and comfy bed, she went to the lodge.

If Gage Stanton was going to begin shadowing her that morning, she wanted to be ready.

However, as she walked along the quiet corridor, she could hear the murmur of male voices even before she reached the office door.

"—and Rory was just a toddler when her mother and I bought this place," her father was saying. "Never thought it would become as successful as it did. Figure it was her mom that was the reason. Eleanor had a way of making everyone feel welcome."

Rory hesitated in the hallway, resting her hand on the doorjamb. Her mother had died eight years ago, and there wasn't a day since that she didn't miss her. The ache might not be as acute, but it was still there.

She'd accepted that it always would be. Losing one parent was tragic enough. She was only now beginning to breathe easier where her father was concerned, and it had been two years since he'd received a clean bill of health.

"Did you ever think of selling?"

She winced, easily recognizing Gage's voice, and quickly entered the office. "G'morning," she greeted brightly, not even giving her father a chance to answer the developer's question. "You're up and at 'em early today."

She strode past Gage and dropped a kiss on her father's head, then stood there next to his chair, her hand on his shoulder. She met Gage's eyes, though it took considerable effort.

She didn't know how old he was, but she was guessing somewhere near forty. His dark hair was slicked back from his handsome face, revealing strands of silver near his temples. He'd been clean-shaven the day before, but now his jaw was blurred with faint stubble. Instead of lessening his appeal, it conjured an image of what he probably looked like waking up in bed every morning.

Which was *definitely* not an image she needed

in her head. "I didn't expect you to beat me here to the office. After I left you all after dinner last night, I'm surprised."

"Your other guests are an interesting lot, but a good bottle of whiskey's never been enough to distract me from business the next day, no matter how early."

She hoped that business didn't include trying to acquire Angel River. "They *are* interesting people," she agreed. "Guests come and go here, but each one of them is memorable."

"Exactly what your mama always said." Her dad gave her an approving look as he stood. "And if you'll excuse me, I'll head over to see Chef Bart for my daily oatmeal and leave the two of you to get on with it." On his way out, he straightened one of the framed travel awards hanging on the wall.

She went over to the door and pushed it closed. Now it immediately felt too close inside the room packed with the sofa and chairs along with her dad's oversize desk from two floors up.

She walked back to the armchair her dad had occupied but didn't sit. "My father will never sell Angel River to you." Her words were bold, hiding her shakiness inside, but she kept her voice low and controlled. At least *she* wouldn't be overheard by anyone walking down the hallway.

Gage's brows rose slightly. "I don't recall making an offer to buy Angel River," he said mildly.

Her fingers curled into the worn blue-and-green-plaid upholstery. "But that's what you do," she said. She'd read enough about him to know that. "Buy up struggling properties and turn them into the next jewel in the crown of Stanton Development."

His expression didn't change. "Is Angel River struggling?"

She sank her teeth into her tongue, debating how to answer then cursed herself for not just denying it and being done with it.

Then it didn't matter anyway, because he waved his hand dismissively. "You don't have to answer that." He stood. "I'm not in the market to buy another guest ranch." He smiled. "I'm not sure what to do with the ranch I already *have* bought."

And she wasn't buying his self-deprecation, either.

She changed tacks. "How is your brother this morning?"

His gaze remained steady. "Still pissed at me, I imagine. Or he will be whenever he unearths himself for the day. Is that what you want to know?"

She felt a little ashamed. There'd been obvious tension between him and his brother when she'd left the lodge for the evening. But thanks to the grapevine— i.e., Marni and Megan—Rory had already heard all about the argument between Noah and Gage because of the beer he'd pulled right out of his brother's hand. Marni—on official bartender duty—had carded Noah before serving him. The young man was twenty-two, and to hear the story, he'd been furious and stormed out.

"I heard there was a bit of a disagreement." Understatement of the year. "If there's a legal reason why Noah shouldn't drink, then let me know so we can deal with it without causing a scene next time. Is his ID real?"

"Yes. But he's not long out of rehab, and I'd like him to stay out."

"Is that why he called you his warden?" She hadn't forgotten Gage's curt manner with Noah when they'd arrived.

"I might as well be. He doesn't want to be here. I'm sure you've noticed that already."

"Maybe Noah's feelings about being here will change before too long," she said quietly. Maybe Gage's would, too, but she kept that thought to herself. "Angel River tends to have that effect on people."

"To hear your father, it's not the ranch but the people on it that are the draw."

"Maybe a bit of both." She cleared her throat and brushed her hands together. "So, you're here early this morning, but we might as well get on with things." She glanced at him. "You *did* look at the schedule I gave you last night, didn't you?"

"Yes. Why?"

She shrugged, suddenly wanting to laugh. She was wearing her oldest jeans, held together more by iron-on patches than by thread, a hooded sweatshirt and her oldest pair of boots. He was wearing jeans, it was true. But there was nothing old or worn about them, or anything else he had on. He looked like he'd stepped off the cover of a magazine. She hoped his hand-tooled leather boots survived the morning or he'd brought a spare pair, because there wasn't a shoe store anywhere in the vicinity—not unless you counted the mukluks they sold in the Angel River gift shop.

"No reason," she said blithely and led the way out of the office. "Do we need to stop for some oatmeal for you, too, first?"

He gave a visible shudder. "My mother used to feed me oatmeal every morning when I was growing up. Hate the stuff."

So did she, but she didn't feel a need to tell him that.

"Besides, you stocked the kitchen in the cabin very well. Including coffee. Lots of coffee." A sudden smile hit his eyes, and she nearly tripped over her own feet. He caught her arm. "All right?"

She focused on the carpet as if blaming it. "Just fine."

They went out through the front door, and Rory flipped up her hood against the chill. It wasn't freezing yet, but the way temperatures had dropped lately, it wasn't going to be long.

He didn't seem to be bothered by it, though. "You did bring a coat, didn't you?" She blamed the question on the mom in her. Yes, the cashmere hugging his torso looked great on him but it wouldn't be a match for their weather. "You're going to need more than a sweater if this weather keeps up." The gift shop sold sweatshirts, too, but she had a hard time envisioning him in one. They all bore the Angel River logo—stylized wings and all—across the front.

"Your father told me to come prepared for snow, just in case."

"Smart. I hope we don't get any, though. Not before Thanksgiving, at least."

"Why? Snow means skiing."

"You'd think. But it's not good for business at Thanksgiving when there is snow." She stopped next to the UTV she'd used to take Killy to the bus stop. "I don't know why. Chef's turkey dinner tastes delicious whether snow's on the ground or not. It's just something about the season, I guess." She waited until he'd climbed onto the seat beside her and started the engine. "After Thanksgiving, though? Guests cannot wait for the snow to hit."

"Do you *have* good skiing?"

"If you're into cross-country, it's excellent. But we can't really compete when it comes to downhill." Fortunately, there were plenty of cross-country enthusiasts who sought them out year after year. She hoped this year wouldn't be an exception.

She gunned the engine as they buzzed past the lodge, tires bouncing over the ruts. His shoulder brushed against hers and she drove even faster, wanting a quick end to the ride.

They flew past the big firepit next to the lodge and the rest of the cabins of the main camp. The road evened out slightly when she turned toward the hay barn, but even though that meant they weren't bumping against each other, the damage was done. When she finally parked near the barn door, she quickly hopped out, not waiting to see how quickly Gage followed. She started to rub her shoulder where his shoulder had brushed hers, then realized what she was doing and forced her hand to drop.

She grabbed the cold barn-door handle and pulled. The well-oiled door smoothly slid open, and immediately the three cats sleeping on the floor inside raised their heads.

"Huey, Stewie and Louie," she told Gage, pointing at each one in turn. "They're not very friendly," she warned as they arched their backs and stalked off with tails bushed. "But they keep the mice under control." She headed toward the tractor parked inside with the spreader already loaded up with bales of hay and straw attached to it. "You can climb up and ride on the bales or take the UTV over to the horse barn," she told him. "Your choice." There wasn't room for them both inside the tractor cab.

She was more than a little surprised when he climbed up over the side of the spreader. And that he did it with such ease.

"You don't store the bales in the barn with the horses?"

"We used to. In fact the horses were originally kept in this barn, too. But my father considered it a fire hazard, so he built the horse barn ages ago. It's heated. No need for the insulating factor that the bales offer. Plus it has a sprinkler system. Makes the insurance company happy."

She waited in case he had more questions, but he just sat down on the bales stacked in the spreader, so she climbed in the cab and started the tractor. They rumbled out of the hay barn and slowly circled around the equestrian ring. The tiers of metal bleachers hugging the far curve could accommodate more than a hundred people. Their current guests and staff would only be enough to occupy a third of them.

He raised his voice above the tractor noise. "What do you use the arena for?"

She glanced at him through the cab's back window. "Rodeos," she said loudly. Just not these days. Not since her dad had gotten sick. Now the ring sat empty except as a gathering place for guests heading out on trail and hayrides.

Once they passed the ring, they reached the horse barn. The wide doors on either end of the long structure were already open, and she could see straight through to the pastures on the other side.

Rory drove the tractor right inside and stopped in the wide aisle separating the two rows of horse stalls. She loved the place with its gleaming wood-paneled stalls topped by black pipe. Megan made certain it was meticulously maintained; no one would ever suspect the barn had been built twenty years earlier.

Rory didn't want to think about how long it had been since her father had actually come to the horse barn. How long it had been since he'd been out for a ride.

Gage stood up, pulling her thoughts front and center to focus squarely on him.

The way he was standing on top of the spreader, his head nearly reached the light fixture hanging from the rafters of the steeply pitched roof. "What do you need me to do?"

Stop giving me shivers?

She swiped off her hood, annoyed with herself. What she'd *like* him to do was stay out of her way.

"Start tossing down bales," she told him. "And don't throw out your back while you're doing it." Not that he looked in danger of that, but she'd learned the hard way with overenthusiastic guests who'd helped with the chore in the past.

Naturally, he of the cashmere sweater and all manner of gorgeousness accomplished the task with perfect ease.

There wasn't a great deal of room in the aisle with the spreader blocking it—just enough to walk alongside it and maneuver the bales. After he'd off-loaded half of them, she pulled the tractor forward and they distributed the rest. Then, once the bales were stacked alongside the stalls, he hopped down and she opened the door to the feed room, where the tools were kept, stored neatly on pegs.

She grabbed a pitchfork, shovel, rake and broom. "Ever muck out a stall?"

"No. But I get the general idea."

There was that wry smile again. "You'd be surprised how many people don't." She went back out into the aisle and closed the feed room door with her hip. "The end goal is to save the straw that's not soiled or soaked. The stuff that is gets shoveled up and dumped in the spreader. Do the stalls next to the spreader. Finish them and move the spreader to the next stall, and so on and so forth. Once the stall is clean, we'll spread fresh straw for bedding and fresh hay for feed." She handed him the pitchfork and rake. "Any experience with horses? Livestock in general?"

"I've ridden a time or two."

Which could mean anything. People either overestimated their abilities or underestimated them. It was fairly rare for a guest to be perfectly honest and accurate. And she didn't want to make assumptions just because he could toss a hay bale as though he'd been doing it all his life. "Well, first off, Megan— she's our wrangler—has already done some of our work for us when she checked the horses earlier—" She broke off at his fleeting expression. "What?"

"It's really early now."

She almost laughed. And it was probably a little cruel of her to gleefully anticipate the day when he shadowed her as she helped Bart in the kitchen.

That was early.

Maybe by then Gage would decide he wasn't so interested in how a guest ranch operated. Maybe he'd decide he and his brother didn't need to stay there for the next six weeks.

The thought was appealing until she thought about having to refund all that money he'd already paid.

To say it'd leave a dent in the bank account was putting it mildly.

On one hand, she might sleep better with him gone, but her personal convenience was a high price for Angel River to pay.

"This is nothing. At least it's already light," she told him. "By the middle of next month, it'll be dark at this time of the morning. Anyway, as I was saying, Megan already moved the horses out to pasture." She entered the first stall and walked to the far side to glance in the water buckets hanging on the wall. "And she's already filled the water, so that's one less thing we have to do." Even though she knew she didn't need to, she looked in the feed bucket on the other wall. It, too, had been cleaned.

He glanced down the aisle. "Twenty-four stalls?"

"Twenty-two. All in use."

"You have more horses than staff."

"At this time of year, yes." She didn't elaborate that they were down several people.

"How much waste does a horse produce?"

She was glad for the turn back to matters other than Angel River staffing levels. "Can be as much as fifty pounds a day. Add in the soiled bedding…" She could see his mind working out the math. "That's why we do this daily. A healthy horse needs a good environment. And a guest ranch without healthy horses isn't much of a guest ranch. They work for us six days a week, so we take care of them."

"I saw in the brochure that you give them Sundays off?"

"Yes."

"And you do this chore every day?" He gestured at the stalls.

"Well, *I* don't do it every single day of the week," she allowed. "Megan and Marni take days, too, including Sundays. And during the summer we have a seasonal crew, which helps give everyone a break."

She waited in case he had more questions or comments, but none came, so she pushed up the sleeves of her sweatshirt and took the pitchfork in hand.

"Easiest way to do this is to work from one corner to the other." She jabbed the tines into the straw, lifting and shaking and turning the pitchfork as she tossed it toward the rear wall. "Don't want to leave anything that's wet." She reached a clump of soiled straw, which she flipped straight into the now-emptied spreader. "Manure management is about a lot more than just shoveling horse crap." She tossed another pile into the spreader and rotated the rake to drag it across the hard-packed earth beneath the straw. "Have to collect it then utilize it when you can or institute a disposal system." She glanced at him as she raked, being careful not to look at him too closely, because every time she did, it was embarrassingly difficult to keep a coherent thought in her head. "Sometimes it has to be stored before that happens. In our case, we're able to use most of it year-round. We have a large compost a ways out beyond the Uptown—"

"That's your corporate area?"

She paused only for a moment to answer. "Primarily. It's good for any sizable group wanting to be housed close together without interference from other guests. My father tell you about it?"

"I studied the map Marni gave us when we arrived."

It was a small matter, but for some reason she was oddly pleased.

She stopped to point at the grilled gate on the exterior wall. Each stall possessed the same emergency gate. The horses could see through it to what went on in the world beyond the barn. It provided them some comfort, because the only times they were ever really happy to be penned up inside was when it was mealtime or there was a blizzard.

"So then you know Uptown is a few miles northwest of the main camp." She was still pointing through the opening. "Can't see from here, but Uptown's just over that ridge." She started scraping and tossing again. "As the crow flies, the compost windrows are between Uptown and Angel camp."

"And Angel camp is where most of the staff lives."

She nodded. Her cabin was in Angel camp. So were her father's, Megan's and Bart's. There were more, but they weren't in use.

"I'd like to see it."

"Angel camp or the compost?"

His gaze slid her way. "Compost."

She was chagrined by the level of her relief. "Then we'll have to fit in a compost tour. A-anyway, like I was saying, we use a lot of what our horses produce. It's either composted—what we can't use for our own gardens gets sold—"

"Good market for it?"

"There's always a market for quality, organic compost." Thank goodness.

"And the rest that isn't composted?"

"Weather permitting, we spread it directly on the fields. That's Seth's call. He runs the cattle operation. If you want to see the typical 'dude' ranch stuff, too, while you're here—"

"Isn't that part of this whole deal?" He looked a little pained. "Playing cowboy?"

"For some," she agreed. "But guest ranching has come a long way since the days of sleeping on a bedroll and going on a roundup. Now, guests come here wanting Bart's farm-to-table food and resort-quality amenities."

"But not high-speed internet," he inserted dryly.

"The ones who really need it to get through their day don't usually bother staying."

His lips twitched slightly. "Touché. So back to the manure. Seth decides whether it gets used now or composted."

She moistened her lips. "Yeah. After we finish the stalls, he'll send someone over for the tractor, dump or spread the stuff, then return the tractor to the hay barn for the next morning."

"Efficient."

"We try. I don't know what sort of setup you'll have on Rambling Mountain—" She hesitated yet again when he gave her a sharp look. "Am I not supposed to know about it?"

"No, I'm just surprised that you do."

She couldn't stop her short laugh any more than she could infuse it with actual humor. She switched the rake out for the shovel, scooping up the pile of debris she'd collected.

She moved past him again and pitched it into the spreader. "Everyone in Wyoming is taking notice. Waiting to see what happens. That ranch you're planning to develop is right on the edge of thousands and thousands of acres of completely undeveloped wilderness. I don't have to tell you how valuable that is. It has everyone worry—*wonder*ing how it'll affect their business." Including them.

"That's a lot of pressure for a little ranch sitting on the side of a mountain."

She held out the pitchfork and nodded toward the stall next door. "You strike me as a man who thrives on pressure."

His fingers brushed hers when he took the handle. "I thrive on lots of things."

Shivers.

She let go of the pitchfork as if it had turned hot. "I hope you thrive on horse manure," she replied, because *surely* there was nothing more effective at killing unwanted shivers than talking about horse poop. "This morning *and* when your Rambling Mountain ranch is up and running. Even a Stanton guest ranch would have to have horses." Then she turned on her heel. "I'm going to get another pitchfork."

Only after she was in the feed room was she able to draw a decent breath. She pressed her palm to her chest, feeling the uneven beat of her foolish heart.

A sound outside the room made her quickly snatch more tools from the pegs and go back out. Megan was there, leaning against the tractor, her arms folded as she openly studied Gage at work inside the stall.

Megan wasn't only Angel River's wrangler. She was Rory's best friend. And there was a glint in her friend's eyes that Rory recognized only too well. Despite Megan's grudge against most of the world's male population, she routinely nagged Rory about

her lack of male companionship. As in Rory's total
sex-life drought.

She jumped in before Megan could say something. "Are you set to take the trail ride this morning?"

Megan's expression was full of mischief. "I
thought maybe you should." Her eyes bounced from
Rory's face to the man working inside the stall. She
didn't even flinch when Gage pitched a heavy wad
of soiled straw in her direction to land unerringly
into the bed of the spreader, missing her by inches.

"If I go on the trail ride, I can't help Frannie with
housekeeping over at Homestead," Rory told her as
if it were breaking news when it was anything but.
Homestead was located in the center of Uptown and
had higher occupancy than anywhere else on the
ranch. It was a lodge in and of itself, though she
considered it to have less character than the main
lodge. "Are you saying *you* want to change sheets
and dust shelves?" She knew Megan would sooner
have her fingernails peeled off. She hated cleaning
even her own cabin. And she particularly disliked
working alongside Frannie.

But Megan evidently wasn't going to give in
quickly, because she gave an expressive eye roll toward Gage. "But maybe our newest guest would
enjoy the ride." She wasn't going to win awards for
subtlety any faster than she'd win one for housekeeping.

"I should introduce you." Rory reentered the stall

she'd been cleaning and looked through the vertical pipes on the upper portion of the partition wall to see that Gage had already cleared two-thirds of the next stall. At the rate he was going, he'd have his stall finished before hers. "Gage Stanton, this is our wrangler I mentioned earlier. Megan Forrester, Gage Stanton."

"*Head* wrangler," Megan corrected with a faint smile.

"She's in charge of the seasonal crew," Rory clarified. "She keeps all the other activities on track, too, not just ones involving the horses."

Gage pitched another load into the spreader. "Sounds like you all wear more than one hat."

"More so in the past year," Megan said bluntly before Rory could telepathically stop her. "The spa director. The office administrator. Head of housekeeping. Everyone's stretched too thin."

It wasn't that Rory intended to hide anything from Gage, exactly. For all she knew, her father had already told him all of this. "It's a temporary bump." She tried to send Megan a mental nudge to hush.

But since Rory was not in the least telepathic, she knew the effort would be useless.

"Maybe Gage's brother would like to join the trail ride," she suggested brightly, hoping to change the subject. She glanced through the bars again toward Gage. "Does Noah enjoy horses? Does he ride?"

"I doubt it." He gave her a quick glance, looking like he regretted the terse comment. He stood the fork on its tines and crossed his arms atop the handle. "I should know whether he likes horses or not, but I don't." He looked toward Megan. "Do you have a big group going out this morning?"

"Only six, so there's plenty of room. And it doesn't matter a lick whether he's ever been around a horse in his life." She pushed away from the side of the tractor as if she'd suddenly tuned in to the mental messages Rory was sending. "I'll just go on over and ask him and leave the two of you to your... work." She gave Rory a wicked look as she turned to leave. "Nice meeting you, Gage."

As much as Rory had wanted Megan to move along, once she had, the barn suddenly felt secluded and too intimate. She avoided Gage's gaze like the coward she was, ducking her head over her pitchfork as she scraped the last bits of muck into a small pile. "You'll want to go on a trail ride yourself at some point. In fact, you could go this morning like Megan said." She hated that she sounded overly cheerful. "Experience isn't necessary, and seeing the place from horseback is one of the best ways to experience it." Their ATV tours were wildly popular, but Rory personally preferred horseback.

"Do you ever go out on the rides yourself?"

"If we have a particularly large group, I help out." She exchanged the pitchfork for the shovel and scooped up the pile, carrying it out to the spreader. "I've been on horses most of my life, but Megan is the one with the real touch with our guests."

She saw that his stall was spotless, with all of the clean straw loosely piled in one corner. "Nice job."

"Cleaning up crap. Been doing it most of my life."

She couldn't help smiling. It was suddenly much too easy to like him, and since she wasn't ready to trust him, that wasn't necessarily a good thing. "Well, now you spread the straw back around, toss in more from the fresh bale—some stalls'll take a whole bale, some'll take less—until there is a nice, good, fluffy bed."

He began deftly pitching the straw about. "What about the hay?"

"We'll put it on the wall next to the water buckets. That's one of the reasons for the concrete apron around the perimeter of each stall," she said.

"You don't stick it in a rack or bag?"

She shook her head. "Leaving it on the ground gives them a natural position to eat. It's also a good reason for checking the stalls as often as we do. Same reason we use water buckets instead of automated systems. Gives us more opportunity to personally attend to the horse. See how his digestion is going, if you know what I mean."

"This guy's digestion seemed just fine to me," he said with half a smile.

"That's a good thing." She took two flakes from the straw bale and went back into the stall with him, handing one to him. "This is Moonbeam's stall." She quickly pulled apart her flake, tossing the fresh, fragrant straw around as she automatically backed her way to the stall door. "He's a big boy, makes a big mess and likes a thick bed. It'll take a fair—" She broke off when her hand collided with Gage's. "Sorry," she mumbled, feeling about as mature as a third grader discovering the boy sitting next to her was cute.

He glanced at her. "Occupational hazard."

She dammed off the flush threatening to flow through her veins and managed a brief laugh. She cast the rest of the straw and backed out entirely, then crouched to pull several more sections from the bale where it naturally separated. She tossed the flakes toward Gage. "Like I was saying, it'll take a fair amount of straw. So grab whatever you need." She glanced up at him as she rose.

His brown gaze seemed to engulf her, and his eyebrow peaked slightly. "Thanks for the offer."

And her flush spilled right around the dam.

Chapter Four

"What happens if it rains on the carnival?"

Rory looked over to Killy where he stood in the open doorway of their cabin. He was looking up at the bleak sky. "Then it rains." She set his dinner plate on the table. "Close the door and come and eat."

Shoulders slumping slightly, he closed the door, immediately cutting off the bite of cold breeze that had been blowing inside. "The costume parade is outside," he said.

"They'll move it inside if they need to." She filled his glass with milk and set it beside his plate. "Don't worry so much. Halloween carnivals sometimes get rained on. Particularly around here. They'll have a plan."

He sat down in the spot opposite hers and propped his elbow on the table, his cheek on his palm. "But—"

"Killy," she cut him off gently, but firmly. She picked up her own fork. "*Eat.* The carnival is the day after tomorrow. Who knows what the weather will be by then."

"But—"

"Killian." She tapped his plate with the fork. He needed to eat dinner then finish his worksheets from school, have a bath and go to bed. Mornings started early around here.

He sighed mightily, then picked up his fork and jabbed it into the mac and cheese that he usually loved, even when she was the one who prepared it. Fortunately, after the first bite, he sat up and looked slightly more interested in eating than worrying about the carnival. Satisfied, she stabbed her fork into her salad.

"Are we gonna live here forever and ever?"

A slice of cucumber fell off her fork as she looked over at him. "Where did that come from?"

He squirmed on his chair and shoveled more noodles into his mouth. "Damon says Astrid says we're all gonna have to leave," he said around his food.

"Don't talk while you're chewing," she said automatically. "And why does Astrid think we're all gonna have to leave?"

"'Cause Frannie says so."

Rory stifled her annoyance. "And why does Frannie say so?"

"'Cause we don't got good business now."

"Don't *have*," she corrected. "And we're fine as far as our business goes." It wasn't strictly true, but she was more worried about her father's state of mind than the state of the business. Which wasn't something her child needed to know.

"But—"

"But nothing, Killy. You and me and Grandpa? This is our home."

"Forever and ever?"

She wanted to tell him yes. When she'd been his age, forever and ever had seemed such a certainty. But life had shown her otherwise.

Still, he was only six. Santa, the Easter Bunny and the Tooth Fairy were still fixtures in his world, and she hoped that they would be for some time to come. "Forever and ever," she assured him, then pointed her fork at his plate again. "Now finish your food."

His worry evidently assuaged for now, he did just that, shoveling in forkfuls with his usual voracious speed, finishing two helpings plus his salad before Rory had made it through her own salad. He clattered his dishes into the sink then spread his worksheets on the table across from her while she finished eating. Then it was bath; then it was bed.

And then, finally, all was quiet.

She went back downstairs and fixed herself a cup of hot chocolate, wrapped a heavy shawl around her shoulders and went out to sit on the porch that ran the full length of the cabin. In layout, it was similar to the Brown cabin where she'd put Gage and Noah, though hers and Killy's was a lot more cluttered.

Such was life with her child, and she wouldn't change it for the world.

She plumped the plaid pillow on the sturdy rocking chair on her porch and sat down, exhaling deeply.

She didn't bother with turning on the light. She knew every inch of the cabin and its immediate surroundings with her eyes closed tight. And despite the distance to the main camp, she could see a glow in the sky from the bonfire burning down at the beach-like clearing next to the river.

She stretched out her feet and propped her woolly slippers on the porch rail. She wondered if Gage had joined the rest of the guests for the fire. Or had he stayed closer to his own cabin, where she knew there'd be a much smaller fire burning in the firepit near the lodge?

That morning, they'd spent two hours mucking the stalls, which was actually less time than it usually took. Neither one of them had said much as they'd worked. She'd expected him to pepper her with questions, but he hadn't.

If anything, he'd seemed preoccupied as he'd methodically worked his way through the stalls at a faster clip than even she could manage.

After that task, though, instead of accompanying her to Uptown, he'd excused himself on the pretext that he had to take care of some business.

Privately, she figured he'd had enough cleaning chores for one day. He was a good enough sport when it came to shoveling horse manure, but dusting shelves was probably not in his nature any more than it was in Megan's.

Rory hadn't seen him again that day until lunch, which had been served at the cookhouse. Like her, he'd changed his clothes after the mucking chore, and Rory could only hope that she hadn't been as obvious with her ogling as Willow had been. What the man did for a pair of black jeans and a plain white shirt ought to be illegal.

There'd been no sign of Noah at lunch, and she knew Megan hadn't been able to get him out on the morning trail ride. She wondered if he'd surfaced for dinner and the bonfire.

Rory had spent the afternoon with Gage in the office while she put in Bart's supply order. Then she'd given him a general overview of their organizational structure while she worked on the following day's payroll.

She felt certain that all of the Stanton properties would have state-of-the-art technology, but to his credit, he hadn't acted condescendingly when it came to what she knew was an antiquated system.

Nevertheless, she'd been grateful as all get-out when she'd had to leave to pick up Killy from the bus stop.

There was a gust of wind, and she tightened her shawl, cradling the hot mug in her other hand. She wished she felt more content. As content as she had when she'd first returned to the ranch after her divorce. Before Killy was born. Before her dad's cancer. Before she'd needed to take over as Angel River's manager.

When she heard the crunch of footsteps on gravel, she peered into the inky darkness in front of her. It was probably Megan, coming by with her own nightly cup of hot chocolate, though hers would be the boozy variety.

"Thought you'd still be down at the bonfire," Rory told her.

"Gave up bonfires back in my college days," a voice—most assuredly *not* Megan's—replied.

Rory yanked her slippered feet down from the rail and nearly spilled hot chocolate all over herself as a result. She still couldn't see the speaker, but she'd know his voice anywhere now.

She watched Gage's shadowy form solidify as he came closer. "This is a surprise."

"Hope it's not an unwelcome one."

"Of course not," she lied.

"Spoken like the best of resort managers, determined to never offend a guest."

"Careful where you walk, though. There's a tree stump I wouldn't want you knocking into."

He stopped on the other side of the rail, his face a pale blur in the night. "Mind if I join you?"

"Of course not," she repeated, lying yet again. "Have a seat." She gestured at the twin rocker next to hers and ignored her edgy shivering when he stepped up onto the deck and lowered himself into the chair.

She could tell he was finally wearing a jacket, but otherwise it was too dark to see much detail. She held up her mug. "Can I get you something hot to drink?"

"That's probably another offer just to be polite, but yeah. I'll take anything. It was colder walking up here than I expected."

His rueful honesty was annoyingly charming.

She gathered her shawl around her and stood. "If you want to come inside where it's warm—"

"Nah." He stretched out his long legs, sighing a little, as though in relief. "It's a nice night."

Another gust of wind blew past, sending the long, tangling fringe of her shawl slapping across him.

She laughed a little, despite herself. "I noticed." She gathered up the end of the shawl. "I'll just be a minute or two. You prefer coffee or hot chocolate?"

"Right now, plain hot water would work."

She laughed again and quickly went inside. If she had to lean back weakly against the door for a moment, nobody needed to know but her. When the door suddenly rattled under a gust of wind, though, she jumped away from it like she'd been bitten and hurried into the kitchen.

She poured more milk into the saucepan she'd used earlier and set it back on the stove to heat, then nipped into the bathroom. The shawl was ancient.

Her woolly slippers were even older. The fact that she stopped to swipe some clear gloss over her lips embarrassed her so much that she grabbed some tissue and wiped it right back off again.

He's a guest, she reminded herself sternly. A guest's stay always, always ended.

She returned to the kitchen and hurried the hot milk along by turning up the flame. She scooped some of the melted chocolate mixture she'd made earlier into a clean mug, and as soon as the milk was steaming, she stirred it in.

Then, mindful of Megan's preferred recipe, she pulled out a bottle of Irish cream and a clean teaspoon. She topped off her own mug with more hot milk, then—since she didn't have a tray handy— just set everything on a wood cutting board and carried it out the door, hitting the light switch with her elbow along the way.

Gage hadn't changed positions. He was squinting slightly in the sudden light from the fixture next to the door.

She set the board on the narrow table between the two chairs and handed him his mug before sitting back down. "Wasn't sure if you want some more comfort or not," she explained when he eyed the bottle of liqueur. Then she felt a quick stab. His brother had a drinking problem and she, of all people, should know better. Her ex-husband had been a recovering alcoholic. "Sorry if that was insensitive."

In answer, he spun the cap off the bottle and

dumped a shot into his mug. Then he looked inquiringly at her, and she had an oh-well sort of moment and held out her mug. He poured again, then recapped the bottle. He stirred his hot chocolate with the spoon, which he handed to her when he was done.

Her fingers brushed his when she took the spoon, and it clattered a little as she stirred. She quickly tapped it against the edge of the cup and dropped it onto the cutting board.

Then she dragged her shawl back up over her shoulders and stared blindly at the glow of the distant bonfire. "I hope you enjoyed Chef's dinner this evening."

"I don't usually care for fish that much, but it was excellent. If I could figure out a way to steal Chef Bart from you, I would."

She startled only to realize he was smiling slightly.

Expecting a reaction.

"Go ahead and try." She subsided in her chair again. "He's pretty loyal to my father, so it'll cost you a good bit."

Gage's smile widened before it was hidden by the mug he lifted to his mouth. When he was done, he propped his drink on the flat arm of the rocker. "I don't remember the last time I drank hot chocolate. Spiked or otherwise." His boot shifted slightly and the chair gave a soft, comfortable creak as it rocked gently. "Much less sat in a rocking chair." He made a sound. "Almost as good as a hammock."

"For relaxation, you mean?" She'd set her own chair into faint motion without even thinking about it. "I prefer a rocking chair," she admitted. "Last time I tried a hammock, I ended up flipping right out of it. Earned a mouthful of dirt." She looked back at him. "*Not* relaxing at all," she said dryly.

The corners of his lips lifted. Despite the porch light, his dark eyes were still too shadowed to see his expression. "Last time I was actually in a hammock was on my honeymoon."

The hot chocolate suddenly tasted bitter, and she automatically looked at his hand even though she knew better than to expect every married man in the world to wear a wedding ring. Jon certainly hadn't. At the time, his reasoning had been safety at work. As a metal artist, he'd done a lot of welding.

As an artist, he'd done a lot of things—mostly other women.

The fingers Gage had curled around the thick mug were devoid of rings. So were those on his right hand.

"If you're married, you could have brought your wife," she said stiffly. "We have a larger cabin avail—"

"Think her present husband would've had an objection or two to that."

Her relief was nearly comical.

But why should she care whether he was married or not? It was none of her business.

Trying to ignore the war between her mind and her emotions, she took another healthy sip of hot chocolate, forgetting all about the added liqueur. She managed not to cough as the heat barraged her throat.

"We divorced a long time ago," he said. "Janie's a good kid, but we never should've gotten married in the first place." He picked up the Irish cream and uncapped it again, adding another measure to his mug.

Rory shook her head when he glanced at her. "I'm fine," she managed hoarsely. "Did you—" she had to clear her still-burning throat "—have kids?"

"Thank God, no."

She thought of Killy sleeping in his room upstairs. "My son was the one good thing that came of my marriage." She couldn't believe the words actually came out of her mouth.

"What happened?"

She wound her fingers in the fringe on her shawl.

"Too personal of a question?"

She opened her mouth, not sure what to say even though she'd been the one to bring up this particular subject.

"Don't worry," he continued. "My staff routinely reminds me that I ask them."

She latched on to her chance to change the topic. "How many people do you have working for you?"

"In my Denver office or altogether?"

"Either." She waved her hand. "Both."

"Thirty-two in the office. Overall, depending on the season, the number varies between two and three thousand. Give or take a couple hundred."

"I didn't realize Stanton Development was that large," she managed faintly. She hadn't researched him anywhere *near* well enough.

He shrugged. "No reason why you would. I'm a developer at heart. Once my projects are up and running, I turn them over to management companies. I just happen to own most of them, too. I have very competent people who take care of the day-to-day operations."

"Yet you came here to learn what we have to say?" She shook her head, feeling both bewildered and alarmed. "You could hire anyone you wanted to deal with your Rambling Mountain project."

"I like personally knowing what I'm getting into before I put it in the hands of someone else." He took another sip and flipped up the collar of his leather jacket against another gust of wind. "If I am going to ask someone to shovel horse crap, I want to at least be able to say I know what it feels like."

She eyed him even more closely. "Have you dug a ditch, too? Walked a high-rise girder?" It seemed inconceivable. "Plunged a stopped-up toilet? Delivered room service? Mopped a floor and changed sheets?"

"If I've been able to find a way, I've tried it."

"Then how do you have time to even be the

boss?" She spread her arms wide. "There are only twenty-four hours in a day."

He looked amused. "Now you understand why marriage—hell, relationships in general—don't work for me. Because all I *am* is work. It's the one thing I'm ideally suited for."

She supposed that was how he had to be to achieve his level of success.

She sipped from her mug, vaguely aware that her rocking was more agitated, and decided to change the subject. "Did your brother get out and do one of the afternoon activities?"

Gage patted his chest in an absent sort of way, as if he were looking for something. "My brother didn't get out of bed until just before dinner." His hand dropped again. "As a warden, I'm not doing that good of a job."

"You're not really his warden, though."

"He had a choice of me or jail after his latest DUI. What's the difference?" He sounded very, very weary.

She pressed her lips together. Regardless of whether or not he harbored intentions where Angel River was concerned, she couldn't help feeling for him. "Is there something I can do to help?"

"Take the trail ride tomorrow," he suggested. "He'll go if you do."

She wasn't sure why that would make a difference. But since she'd gone and offered assistance, she couldn't very well refuse now. "I'll need to switch a schedule or two, but I can do that."

"Great." He suddenly drained his mug and stood, as if he'd achieved whatever it was that he'd walked all the way up there to accomplish. "Thanks for the drink." He stepped off the porch. "Was as good as my mother used to make."

She managed a bemused "thank you," but he was already walking away.

"You said she was going to be here," Noah said under his breath. "Was that a lie just to get me to come?"

Gage inhaled the crisp morning air, reminding himself that biting off Noah's head wouldn't accomplish anything. "No. And I expect Rory will be here. There are two more horses already saddled over there." The saddle creaked beneath him when he shifted, nodding toward the horses still waiting near the fence of the riding ring where they'd all been led by Megan after they'd saddled up.

The tall wrangler was giving a thumbnail course in basic horsemanship before they headed out, and Gage could tell she was gauging for herself how comfortable he and Noah—as the newcomers— were on their mounts. It'd been a while since Gage had been on horseback, but aside from the fact that he was a helluva lot older than the last time, it was sort of like riding a bike.

Noah's ease on his horse, though, was a complete

surprise. Of course, when he'd asked his brother about it, Noah had just given him one of his typical smart-ass responses.

The two of them had a long stay at Angel River ahead of them. If Gage had to put up with Noah's present attitude for much longer, he was afraid he'd haul Noah back to jail himself.

He was already second-guessing his decision not to drag Noah out of bed the previous day. His brother was supposed to be working during his "sentence" with Gage.

But after their set-to the night they'd arrived, Gage hadn't had the stomach to ruin his morning with Rory.

Then he saw Noah's attention perk and followed his brother's gaze.

Rory was striding toward them.

The breeze had her long hair blowing around her shoulders in a tangle of brown and gold. She was wearing a worn-looking coat in a muddy red shade. Its only real attraction was the fact that it ended at her hips, where equally worn-looking blue jeans clung to her lithe figure. Her cheeks were ruddy from the cold air, and her eyes were as blue as the sky—at least what could be glimpsed of the sky among the gray clouds scudding across it.

He'd dated women who were far more beautiful. More polished. But as he watched Rory approach, he couldn't recall a single one of their names.

He might not know where Noah had acquired his familiarity with horses, but one sideways glance at him watching Rory, and Gage knew that Noah was feeling the same way as he did.

Not an issue, he reminded himself.

He didn't do relationships and he wasn't there to strike up a fling. He'd learned a long time ago to use the tools at hand. And if Rory's mere presence was enough of an enticement to get his brother out of bed without a battle, Gage would take advantage of that fact.

Megan barely paused in giving her horsemanship spiel when Rory reached the ring and ducked down to slip between the top and middle fence rungs. When she straightened, she gave a quick wave in acknowledgment as she headed toward the taller of the two remaining horses.

The wrangler's words were nothing more than a buzz while Rory checked her saddle. The horse was striking. Chestnut colored with a flaxen mane and tail, she butted her nose against Rory's shoulder until she turned with a smile and pulled something from her pocket. The horse greedily nuzzled her palm, taking up whatever the treat was, and then Rory nimbly swung up into the saddle.

It seemed that she'd hardly taken any notice of the rest of them gathered in the center of the ring, but the second she took the reins and turned the horse slightly, those blue eyes of hers seemed to slam into Gage.

There was just enough time for him to catch her pupils dilating before Noah and his horse cut across his line of sight, heading toward her.

Gage shook off his quick jab of irritation and looked back toward the wrangler, who'd evidently concluded her talk, because she was swinging up into her own saddle.

"All right," Megan said over her shoulder as her horse plodded out of the ring, "next stop will be Angel's Lookout. Your horses know the way, so just remember to keep your heels down and your attention up!"

As if on cue, Gage's mount—Moonbeam of the well-used straw from the day before—lurched forward with no direction from Gage at all. Everyone else's horses seemed to be doing the same.

They knew the way, and they obviously knew how to follow.

Including Megan and Rory, there were only seven riders in their group: Gage, Noah, the chatty Willow and another couple who must have arrived after dinner the night before. He'd only caught their last name. The Coopers were older and seemed excited with everything around them, as if they were on the trip of their lifetime.

Maybe they were.

Moonbeam fell into line behind the couple as they all settled roughly into a single line. Willow was after him, then Noah.

Rory brought up the rear.

Gage couldn't see her without turning around in his saddle. But he was nevertheless aware of her.

Aware in a way he hadn't been in quite a while.

Behind him, he heard Willow's high-pitched chatter as she talked to Noah. Heard the deeper, less enthusiastic responses from his brother.

The distance between each horse grew the farther they got from the main camp. Eventually, the trail began to curve, heading in a different direction than he'd taken the evening before when he'd found his way to Rory's cabin.

He could hear less of Willow now and more of the breeze in the trees. It sounded like water.

Leather creaked. Horseshoes scuffed on rock.

It was lulling in a way he didn't expect.

Eventually, they headed up a steep hillside and the trail curved like a hairpin. Without needing to turn around at all, Gage could see Rory below. She was nearly abreast with Noah, and even as Gage watched, she threw her head back and her laughter floated up to him. Musical. Infectious.

And then he heard something else he hadn't heard in a very, very long time.

Noah laughed, too.

Gage exhaled and looked up at the horse ahead of him.

Not an issue, he reminded himself yet again.

Not an issue at all.

Chapter Five

"It's a beautiful view, isn't it?"

Gage turned away from the precipice overlooking a group of cabins by the river toward Megan.

After reaching Angel's Lookout, they'd all dismounted so everyone could walk farther out beyond the natural outcropping onto the cantilevered deck that had been built into the side of the steep, rocky incline. It was a beautiful view.

No more so, though, than the mountainside view from the ranch he'd purchased on Rambling Mountain.

"It's a good view," he agreed. "The deck's a nice touch. Looks recent."

Megan rested her hands on the top of the deck rail surrounding the hexagonal structure. She was taller than Rory. With fewer curves and, he suspected, more hard-edged nerve.

"It's almost five years old now," she told him. "It was Rory's idea to have it built. The most recent thing that's been added around here." She glanced over to where Rory was talking with Noah. She was pointing out something in the distance, and his brother's head was angled slightly toward her. The Coopers were busy taking selfies with their cell phones, and Willow was hovering well back from the deck, her fear of heights evidently superseding her interest in anything else.

Gage's gaze slid toward Rory again.

"Does that bother you?"

Gage gave Megan a questioning glance.

She jerked her chin toward Noah. "Your brother's obviously got an eye for her."

"Why would it bother me?"

Her smile had a biting sort of edge to it. Not exactly unkind. But definitely not without cynicism.

His smile was probably not much different.

He looked out at the spectacular view again then turned his attention to the deck. He didn't remember it being on the map Marni had given him when he and Noah arrived at the ranch. The brochure must not have been updated in a long time. "What's the space used for?"

Megan shrugged, apparently content to let the matter of Rory and Noah drop. "We've had wedding ceremonies up here. It'll seat about fifty people, but it's a pain in the butt hauling the chairs up here. We do it if it's requested, of course, but it's a helluva lot easier when people coming here to get hitched just use the wedding barn and gardens."

"Get a lot of weddings?"

"A fair amount. Have one coming in a few weeks. Who knows where they'll end up wanting the ceremony. Their party booked all of Uptown. Ten full days of pre- *and* post-wedding festivities planned." She rubbed her thumb and index finger together. "Lot of money in weddings." She made a face. "Lot of work in weddings, too."

"Not to mention the marriage that follows."

She laughed. "Amen to that."

"Anything besides weddings?"

"Oh, yeah." She spread her arms. "We've done yoga sessions during the summer season. Painting classes. There was even a writers' group who rented out Uptown last spring. They held brainstorming sessions out here."

"Only thing that limits the uses here is imagination," he concluded.

"Basically."

"Anyone in the cabins down there?" He pointed toward the roofs far below.

"The Overlook cabins?" She shook her head. "These days they mostly just get used in summer. They're not as well equipped as the cabins in the main camp or Uptown. Little more rustic, you know? But I can remember years when even those places would be booked all year round. And see where the river bends east of the cabins?" She waited until he nodded. "The rapids are just beyond that. So people who are into white-water rafting love the location of the cabins. But the only time it's safe is in the dead of summer, otherwise the water gets pretty wild. That's why we don't let anyone on the river anymore beyond the bridge to the wedding barn unless it's summertime."

"Have you rafted, too?" Rory asked after appearing at their side, miraculously without Noah. She was looking up at Gage, and a tangle of goldish-brown hair kept drifting into her eyes.

He shoved his hand in his pocket, curbing the desire to tuck the silky-looking strands behind her ear. "Yeah." He'd done quite a lot of it back in the day. But that was before his business began demanding all of his time. "Been a long time, though."

"You should come back in the summer," Megan said, and he couldn't miss the quick look that passed between the two women. She didn't seem bothered by it. "We take groups out on the rapids every day," she finished.

"But not at this time of year." He was watching Rory.

She shook her head, her eyes suddenly looking distant. "Not at this time of year," she confirmed. She shot the cuff of her dull-red coat and glanced at her watch. "It's getting on toward lunchtime, Meg."

"Right." Megan clapped her hands once and

quickly moved away from the rail. With a single whistle, the horses who'd been left to roam began circling around her.

Despite her words, Rory didn't head to her own horse, though. Instead she hung back with Gage. "What do you think of our little overlook?"

"Great view." He told her the same thing he'd told Megan. "The deck's a nice touch."

"Thanks." She looked out at the cabins and river below. "This was my mother's favorite place on the ranch. But she wouldn't let my dad build their cabin here because she thought it needed to be shared with everyone who visited."

Her gaze seemed to linger on the vista for a moment before she turned away.

"Her favorite place, but you're sad," he said quietly.

Her brow knitted for a fraction of a second before she gave a quick little shake of her head. "Not at all," she denied. Then she held out one hand in invitation toward the waiting horses and touched his elbow with her other hand, but just as quickly drew back. "Chef has his famous ribs on the menu out at the chuck wagon." Her voice sounded deliberately bright. "And they are *not* to be missed." As if to urge him on, she headed off toward the horses.

He followed more slowly, watching the way Noah materialized at her side, offering her a leg up even though she was more than capable of mounting her horse without assistance.

Gage passed Willow on his way to Moonbeam. "Not one for heights?"

"Hate them," she admitted with a wrinkled nose. Beneath her heavy-handed makeup, she was a pretty girl. "Tig thinks it's silly."

Gage thought it was silly of her to worry about what Tig did or didn't think. "He didn't come riding with you."

She shrugged one shoulder, trying and failing to look unconcerned. "He had business to take care of."

It didn't matter that the girl was at the ranch with a married man who was old enough to be her father. There was still something sadly sympathetic about her. "Need help up?"

Her expression brightened. "Yes, please."

He walked over and linked his hands together just as Noah had done for Rory. Willow placed her expensive cowboy boot in his palms. She was excruciatingly thin. It took no effort at all to boost her up.

She gave him a beaming smile that seemed to stay there for the duration of the ride back down to the main camp. There, they left the horses in Megan's hands and walked over to the chuck wagon for ribs.

Gage followed along with the rest, returning Bruce Cooper's rueful smile as the other man stretched his legs with feeling. "Don't remember if this place has a whirlpool or not."

Rory overheard him. "We do." Her smile skated

over both Gage and Bruce. "Two, actually. One at the lodge and one at the Uptown camp."

"Thank goodness." Missy Cooper caught up to her husband. She was rubbing her backside. "I used to ride horses when I was a little girl. Why is it that even though I have so much more padding than I did then, it hurts more now?"

"The universe's practical joke on us." Bruce gave her a wink as he dropped his arm around her shoulders.

"How about you?" Rory asked Noah. "Feeling saddle sore yet?"

Noah shook his head. "From a little ride like that? Nah."

"Great," Rory said cheerfully. "Then you'll be all set for our daylong ride next weekend. I'm going to put your name down on the list as soon as I get back to my office."

Gage tucked his tongue in his cheek, looking away from his little brother to keep from laughing at the chagrin Noah couldn't hide.

He joined the line in front of the covered wagon with its long table loaded with food protruding from the back. Beyond the wagon was a cooking pit with two enormous blackened pots hanging from an iron rack. The rack had the same forged wings as the ones on the ranch entrance sign. It reminded him that he wanted to talk to April and Jed about a new name for the Rad.

April had been his go-to when she'd worked for

him. But he'd ended up losing her to Jed Dalloway, who'd been running the ranch for Otis Lambert before he died. Now she and Jed were living in the ramshackle ranch house wallowing in wedded bliss, and they were his partners in turning the Rad into something profitable.

"Who did the ironwork?" he asked the chef when it was his turn in line.

Bart followed his gaze then served him several glistening ribs. "Better ask Rory that," he said. "Corn bread and beans?"

Gage nodded absently. Once his plate was full, he turned toward the weathered picnic tables arranged under several trees. He sat down next to the Coopers, wincing a little as he sat.

It turned out that Bruce Cooper wasn't the only one who could use a hot soak.

Rory eyed the guests as they settled themselves around the picnic tables. The Coopers and Gage sat together at one. Willow and Tig, who'd been at the chuck wagon when they'd arrived, joined Marni and Chef Bart at another.

Even though there was plenty of room at either table, Noah had chosen to sit at the third table, alone. He had a plate of food in front of him that he seemed to have no interest in eating. Instead, he just watched his brother with a vaguely sulky look on his young, handsome face.

She picked up a jug and a couple of glasses and

headed toward him. "You don't have anything to drink, Noah." She set the glasses on the table and held up the jug. "How about some cider?"

"Is it hard?"

"Nope," she said cheerfully and filled one of the glasses with the deep, golden juice. "Just good old-fashioned apple. Chef Bart makes it himself every year."

She set the jug in the center of the table and retrieved her own plate of food before sitting across from him.

She thought she saw surprise in his blue eyes—at least enough to replace the sulkiness for a second.

He hadn't filled his glass yet, so she did it for him. "Just one drink," she encouraged the same way she would have with Killy.

Then she picked up one of the ribs on her plate and began eating.

Before long, she heard Noah's grumbled sigh as he took a sip from his glass.

She didn't act as if she even noticed, and eventually, he tried the ribs.

She hid a smile. It really was like dealing with Killy. Before she'd made it halfway through her own plate of food, Noah had finished all of his and gone back for more. When he sat down again, the sulky look seemed to have been retired altogether.

At least for now.

She refilled his glass and looked past his shoulder to see Gage watching them. It seemed to take a mammoth effort just to look away.

Now she felt too warm. She unbuttoned her coat and focused more narrowly on her tablemate. She didn't want to be getting too warm over any man, much less a *guest* who had the capacity to buy them out if he took it into his mind to talk her father into it.

"So, Noah, tell me more about when you played polo." He'd mentioned it during the ride up to the lookout. "Were you in college?"

He nodded. "Played when I was in high school, too."

Noah made it sound as if high school polo teams were commonplace, and she couldn't help but laugh. "Polo most definitely was *not* on the roster of sports at the high school I went to."

"It was a private school." He wiped his fingers on the bright red bandanna-patterned napkin.

"Did your brother go to the same school?" She cursed herself even as the words came out. Not only because it proved how miserable her self-control was when it came to keeping her mind off Gage, but because Noah immediately shut down.

"No."

"Did you play other sports?" she asked quickly. Brightly. Hoping to rectify her mistake. She gave him a coaxing smile. "Or were you chasing girls?"

The look he gave her underscored his resemblance to Gage. Luckily he seemed to relax enough to ask a question of his own. "Where was your high school?"

"In Wymon. It's the closest town to the ranch here."

"Never heard of it."

"Not surprising," she said wryly. "Population is less than eight hundred people. Wymon has an elementary school, which my son attends now, a middle school and a high school that share the same building, five churches and no bars."

He shuddered visibly. "What about college?"

"I went to art school, actually."

He raised his eyebrows. "You *paint*?"

He made it sound as if she'd told him she danced naked on the moon every third Friday. "Ceramics, actually. Pottery. Clay. That sort of thing."

"So what're you doing in *this* place?"

"It's my home," she said mildly.

"Yeah, but—" He leaned forward. "What do you do all day? Don't you get bored?"

"We're too busy to get bored." Not as busy as they ordinarily were, but she brushed aside the nettlesome fact. "What do *you* do all day?" She grinned. "When you're not enjoying all the comforts here at Angel River, that is."

He shrugged again. "Nothing that matters."

She folded her arms on the table in front of her and leaned toward him. "What *does* matter to you?" Out of the corner of her eye, she couldn't help but be aware of Gage rising from his seat.

Noah seemed to have noticed, too, and didn't answer her question. He couldn't stop watching Gage any more than she could.

Gage carried his tin-style plate over to the chuck wagon and dropped it in the container for dirty dishes.

When he started their way, Rory tried to blame her shiver on her coat falling open but knew better.

She hoped that this particular affliction wore off soon. She wasn't a masochist. She didn't relish another six weeks of butterflies and hypersensitive shivers every time he got within ten feet of her.

He stopped next to their table, obviously taking note of Noah's nearly empty plate. "Glad to see you finally ate something."

As if controlled by a light switch, Noah's expression turned pugnacious.

Hoping to stave off an argument between them, Rory quickly stood. "Nobody can resist Chef Bart's ribs," she said loudly. "Isn't that right, everyone?" She glanced around at the rest of the guests, and by some divine intervention, they seemed to grasp her intention.

To a one, they began clapping and cheering for the chef, who blushed at the sudden accolades.

"Only thing to top it off is dessert," Marni added as she rose and went over to the chuck wagon. She pulled out a container and flipped off the lid to reveal a display of enormous cookies individually wrapped in cellophane. She offered Noah first choice. "Plenty of options," she coaxed. "My faves are the oatmeal raisin. Chef Bart dries his own grapes, if you can believe it. Best raisins you'll ever taste."

While Marni continued extolling the glories of Chef's cookie selection, Rory took her plate over to the plastic bin and set it inside. Gage followed her.

She glanced at her watch. "There's still time for a few hours in the office. I'll be working on a couple of inquiries that came in last night." Hopefully she could convert them into actual bookings.

She couldn't help being disappointed when Gage declined, even though she'd expected him to. She doubted that he needed a lesson in processing reservations now that she knew he maintained an interest in the projects he developed. It was probably one of those tasks he prided himself on having tried at least once.

"All right, then." She looked over at Noah. "Be sure to participate in one of the afternoon activities."

"Skeet shooting or rock climbing," Marni interjected. "Can't go wrong with either one."

"Or a session with me in the bakery," Chef Bart reminded. "Soufflés."

"There you go." Rory just couldn't help herself. She looked from Noah to Gage. "Hopefully something whets everyone's interest. And if not, there's nothing wrong with relaxing at the lodge with a book or a game of horseshoes."

"Or a cold beer," Tig said with a hearty chuckle.

Pretending she didn't see Noah's grimace, Rory said her goodbyes and escaped.

As soon as she set off on foot toward the lodge, though, Gage fell into step right alongside her.

She shoved her fists into her coat pockets, watching him from the corner of her eye. "Thought you were giving the office a pass."

"I am." He gave that now-familiar pat at his chest before he dropped his hand. "I need to take care of some business with my lawyer."

"Every time we have a lawyer here as a guest, I have nightmares of being sued for something trivial. Like the baking lesson with Chef Bart is a sham 'cause the lawyer's soufflé fell flat."

Gage laughed.

She was almost getting used to the shivers slipping delectably down her spine every time he did so.

She ducked her head slightly and walked a little faster.

He didn't have to make any effort to keep up. "Thanks, by the way, for coming on the ride this morning."

"Sure. Noah rides very well." Deep inside her pockets, she curled her fingers into her palms. *Just leave it at that, Rory.*

She repeated the admonishment to herself in time with her boots hitting the gravel road. *Leave...it...*

She sneaked a look at Gage from beneath her lashes.

Leave...it...

"He even played polo." So much for leaving it.

If she'd expected him to be surprised she knew that, maybe even a little jealous, she was disappointed.

"Which is the reason he rides well," was all Gage said.

In a neutral voice.

An I-don't-really-give-a-damn voice.

She kicked a pebble out of her path and watched it skitter and bounce until it came to land on the side of the pathway. "It's obvious you've ridden horses more than just a time or two, yourself," she said. "Did you play polo, too?"

"No." He didn't elaborate.

It was like pulling teeth. And she'd never enjoyed dentistry.

As she struggled to come up with something to say, she spotted Megan on one of the UTVs heading away from the lodge. Divine intervention. "There's Megan. I need to go over some stuff with her." It wasn't an outright lie. There was always something she needed to go over with every single person on the Angel River crew. "Good luck with your lawyer."

She barely waited for a response before she waved to get Megan's attention and ran after her.

She was breathless once she reached the UTV. "Hey." She propped her hands on her hips and hauled in a deep breath.

Megan had a definite glint in her eye. "Running from temptation always makes a person out of breath."

"I don't know what you're talking about." Of course, Rory went and ruined that particular pronouncement by sneaking a look back in Gage's direction.

He was too far away to see his expression, but he'd nearly reached his cabin. His stride was long. Ground-eating. All business.

He didn't look her way as he reached the deck surrounding the cabin and disappeared inside.

She felt her breath leak out of her.

"He's been here only a few days," Megan said. "What're you going to be like after he's been here two months?"

"He's not staying two months."

"Okay. A month and a half," Megan allowed. Her voice was tart. "Huge difference. Astronomical."

"Oh, be quiet."

Megan looked at the imaginary watch on her wrist. "Let's see. October's kaput."

"Don't let Killy hear you say that. He's been talking about nothing but the Halloween carnival in town."

Her attempted change of subject was lost on Megan. "Gorgeous Gage will be here until after gobble-gobble day. I give you—" She squinted as if in great thought. "Three weeks. Less if you dress up as something sexy for the bonfire on Saturday."

Rory climbed into the UTV beside Megan. "For

what?" she asked even though she knew better than to encourage her friend.

"Before you're knocking boots."

Rory rolled her eyes, trying to squash the images that suddenly filled her head. "I don't get involved with our guests," she said severely. "You know that."

"Yeah, not since Jon." Megan ignored the stony look Rory gave her. "You told me yourself. Gage isn't the typical garden-variety guest."

Rory pressed her fingertips to her temples to stop the pain suddenly throbbing behind her eyes. "Can you just drive or something? At least *look* like we have important things to take care of?"

The UTV lurched into motion, but instead of continuing to drive away from the lodge and the adjacent cabins, Megan made a wide, loopy U-turn. "I think it's fairly important for you to venture out of your self-imposed sex desert."

Rory dropped her hand. "Megan!"

The other woman just shrugged, unrepentant.

"I could say the same about you," Rory grumbled. "And if you expect *me* to put on a costume for the bonfire Saturday night, then you'd better do so as well. And that does *not* include showing up like Annie Oakley, because that's your usual look. And *where* are we going right now?"

"Forgot I need to drop off the firewood." Megan jerked her head to indicate the split logs in the cargo box. "And I'm *not* the same as you, because *this*

Annie Oakley freely admits that the only thing she thinks men are good for is a good scr—"

Rory lifted her hand, cutting her off. "Yes, you've told me that numerous times." She was already stepping out of the vehicle next to the firepit before they came to a full stop. She grabbed the logs and deftly stacked them near the pit, then swung right back into the utility vehicle.

Megan hit the gas even before Rory's rear hit the seat. She zipped toward the road between the lodge and the cabins. "Whereas you, missy, still believe in all that happily-ever-after stuff. In fact, I think you should dress up like a bride Saturday night."

Rory tossed up her hands. "A minute ago, I was merely sex-starved!"

As Megan snorted with laughter, Rory spotted Gage standing in the doorway of his cabin.

Close enough to have heard every darn word.

Chapter Six

"Cap'n 'Merica saves the day!" As Rory turned off the engine, Killy hopped out of the truck, the buckle on his safety belt clanking hard against the door frame.

He didn't notice.

He was too busy running around, brandishing his cardboard shield and enjoying the swish of the superhero cape that he'd won in the costume parade at the Halloween carnival. He climbed atop a tree stump that was almost as tall as he was, hopped onto the corner of the patio deck, then back down again.

She was still gathering their belongings from the back seat of the truck—including his stuff that she'd told him to carry in himself—when he disappeared around the corner of the cabin, though she could still hear his enthusiastic whoops.

"That's a lot of energy."

She dropped the armload of gear she'd gathered as she whirled to see Gage standing a few feet away. He'd obviously walked over again. There was no sign of his vehicle or one of the UTVs. "I let him have more Halloween candy than was probably wise," she said, sounding breathless to her own ears.

To hide her reaction, she stuck her head back inside the truck, gathering up her canvas shopping bag, the jacket Killy had abandoned hours ago, the enormous plastic pumpkin filled with his sugary loot from the carnival and the plastic bag containing the goldfish also won in a water pistol game.

"Can I help you with something there?"

"I've got it," she answered brightly and shoved the truck door closed with her hip. She could sense him looking at her and felt her cheeks turning hot. It was pretty annoying. "Have a delicate balance going here." She slipped between him and the truck, heading toward the cabin. "Lose one item and the whole wagon's in danger." From the corner of her eye, she could see Killy now squatting in the road, undoubtedly gathering another fascinating piece of gravel to add to the jumble of rocks he kept in his room. She headed up the steps to the front door, but before she could maneuver enough finger strength to turn the knob, Gage beat her to it.

She felt the brush of his shoulder and hurried

even more quickly inside—so quickly, in fact, that she managed to catch the heel of her boot on the threshold. She didn't even have a chance to gasp or groan or curse her own clumsiness as she pitched forward.

Gage caught her just as the plastic pumpkin bounced against the hardwood floor, shooting out a shower of penny-candy shrapnel. She barely managed to keep from dropping the poor goldfish, and her breath left her in a whoosh when she came up hard against Gage's side. Her canvas bag of groceries was caught between them, and no amount of self-consciousness was enough to keep her gaze from flying up to his.

He may have kept her from falling flat on her face, but she still had the sensation of falling headlong into his intense brown eyes.

"You okay?"

She managed some sort of a croaky sound.

"Squashed, I'm afraid." He reached between them and heat rushed through her veins as his knuckles brushed briefly against her breast. She stared stupidly at the loaf of bread he'd extracted from the bag.

"Mommy!" Killy shoved her from behind and dived to the floor, intent on rescuing his carnival treats. "You spilled my candy!"

Pushed together once more, she and Gage both winced at the sharp edges of the cans inside the grocery bag pressed between them. She tried to step back, but her foot landed on Killy's superhero cape, pinning him to the spot and earning her a second, even more outraged yelp from him.

She heard Gage's faint oath, then squealed like a stuck pig when he suddenly wrapped his arm around her waist and lifted her out of the tangle of her son's legs—he surely had sprouted a few extra in the last millisecond—and took a long step right over him.

They could all hear the crunch of hard candies beneath his boots before he set her back on her feet beyond the debris field. Killy's "Mo-om!" contained a new level of despair.

"Killy, it's just a few pieces of hard candy!"

The mulish look he gave her encompassed Gage as well. She'd finally managed to extract her arm from the tangled loop of the grocery bag and dumped it on the couch, then set the poor fish on the mantel. At least she hadn't dropped that, too.

She pointed toward the kitchen. "Go and get a big bowl to put your candy in," she told Killy. "The red one we use when I make popcorn."

He was scooping candy into a pile. "But—"

"Now."

He huffed and got to his feet, then stomped out of the living room.

Rory gave Gage a quick glance. "Sorry. He's overtired and needs a nap, but he's six and there's not a chance in the world I'll get him to take one."

"And I crunched his—" he'd crouched down to pick up one of the wrappers "—Spicy Hots. Major crime. Used to eat these things by the pound when I was a kid. Didn't know they still made them."

So had she. "He'll survive. Which is more than I can say for the pumpkin." She scooped up the two pieces of brittle plastic and dropped them on the couch, too. With Gage there, she was very aware of the general untidiness of the room. Killy's discarded school backpack on the floor. Her coffee mug and Killy's unfinished bowl of cereal from that morning still sitting on the table in the dining area.

She could hear her little boy slamming all the cupboard doors in the kitchen even though he knew very well where the large popcorn bowl was. She couldn't fault him too much, though. She'd been known to slam a door or two herself when she was angry.

"Have a seat," she told Gage as she transferred one of Killy's oversize plastic dinosaurs from the cushion of an armchair to the coffee table. "Sorry about the, uh, the—" She broke off at the sound of a loud crash from the kitchen. She'd been about to say "mess," but she sighed. "Insanity," she said instead and hurried into the kitchen.

Killy was sitting on the floor in the midst of several pots and pans, unharmed despite the terrific crash he'd caused.

She crouched beside him. "Where do we keep the popcorn bowl?"

His chin was set, but at her continued silence, he

finally pointed a finger at the cupboard on the other side of the stove. "Over there."

He sounded so disgruntled she had to work hard not to smile. "So why were you looking in here where the pots go?" She picked up a small frying pan and set it back inside the cupboard.

"Dunno."

She rubbed her palm over his sweaty forehead, pushing back his hair and gently directing his focus up to her face again. "If you had carried your candy in like I asked you to in the first place, none of this would've happened," she said calmly. "So you can put the pans back where they belong and get the popcorn bowl or else I'll get the broom and sweep up your candy and whatever I sweep up is going in the trash. So you choose."

He began shoving pans back into the cupboard. It was a disorderly jumble, but she took it as a win and went back into the living room.

Gage was standing near the fireplace, studying the goldfish swimming around in its water bubble.

She watched him for a moment and then flushed all over again when her gaze collided with his in the mirror hanging above the mantel.

Then she caught her own reflection. She'd entirely forgotten her face-painting session at the carnival. Purple-and-green fairy wings radiated from her eyes and met at the center of her forehead in a sunburst of silvery stars.

No wonder he kept staring at her.

"Halloween carnival," she explained, gesturing vaguely at her face. "If I manage not to smear it before tonight, I figure it'll do double duty for the bonfire." She rubbed her hand down her thigh. "You, uh, you plan to go, don't you? Sooner or later you should, and tonight all of the staff'll be celebrating there, too. I have a small group coming in to provide live music."

"Hadn't planned on it. But maybe I need to reconsider." A faint smile was playing around his lips. Lips that were perfectly sculpted. Perfectly shaped. Perfectly—

She cursed her vivid imagination and walked over to the mantel to grab the bag containing the fish. "You should. And your brother, too." She held up the bag, wishing she hadn't mentioned the bonfire at all. "I'd better get this guy in a real fishbowl."

"Do you have one?"

"Somewhere." She pulled open the lowest drawer in the built-in shelves by the fireplace and began poking through it. "From the last time we attempted to keep a fish. Also won from a kids' carnival last spring." The more she talked, the less she had to think about the silly fairy wings painted on her face. "But at the time I figured better a goldfish than a bunny or a chick, which were also prizes."

"Attempted?"

"Voilà." She extracted the bowl and plucked out the can of fish food that had been stored inside it.

"Yeah. He lasted about three weeks. Think we over-fed the poor thing."

"Or maybe it was from trying to keep a goldfish in a bowl like that." Gage's fingers brushed hers as he took the glass sphere from her. "Even goldfish need the proper temperature. Proper water filtration."

"Well." She shook the fish food. "This is all we've got. Has to be better than a zip-top bag." She rounded the couch, avoiding the scattered mess of candy, and went into the kitchen, where Killy was just finishing putting away the pots and pans.

Gage followed and set the fishbowl on the counter. She rinsed it out and then poured the contents of the baggie inside the bowl. The fish darted around its expansive new digs. She bent over, looking closely at it. "All right, Nelson. Hang in there the best you can, right?"

"Nelson?"

She glanced over her shoulder at Gage. "Yeah. Nelson. Something wrong with that?"

His lips were tilted in a faint smile. "Nope. Did you name him, Killy?"

Her son was holding the popcorn bowl. His expression when he looked at Gage was still accusatory. "No." He carried the bowl with him out of the kitchen. "Mommy won him," he said as he went.

Gage looked at her, and she felt the blush creeping up again.

"Water pistol race," she explained. "You know.

Who can fill the balloon the fastest with the water you shoot into the target?"

His smile widened, and she felt more self-conscious than ever. "What, uh, what brought you here this afternoon, anyway? Everything going all right with your visit so far?"

"Had breakfast with your father again."

She hoped her fairy paint hid her worry. "Has he brought you over to the dark side of oatmeal yet? Or did Chef Bart come to your rescue?"

"Actually, Chef Bart let me loose in his kitchen."

"You don't say." She was surprised. "What did you make?"

"Breakfast burritos." He shrugged dismissively. "Throw everything in with some scrambled eggs and cheese and wrap it in a tortilla."

"Breakfast of the gods." She leaned around him to look out at Killy. His legs protruded from beneath the sofa. She wondered what all he would find beneath it besides a piece or two of his precious candy.

She leaned back again, pressing her hands against the countertop behind her. Gage had had breakfast with her father the previous day, too. Before the trail ride. She'd only learned about it when she and Killy had dinner with her dad the night before. "Discuss anything interesting?"

"Nothing in particular. He didn't stay long after his oatmeal. Thought he looked tired."

That answer wasn't exactly a comfort.

"I might be able to help you when it comes to find-ing someone for your spa," he said out of the blue.

She didn't want to admit they needed help with anything. "Oh?"

"Someone I've known for a long time. She owns a string of day spas in Colorado. Successful ones."

Rory began shaking her head before he even fin-ished speaking. "If she owns spas, she wouldn't be interested in working for Angel River as an em-ployee."

"You could contract out the space. Remove that burden from your payroll but still offer spa services. She owns and operates the spa in one of the residen-tial towers I own."

"That's not the way we've done things here."

"Change isn't always a bad thing, you know."

How many times had she said that to her father? And then he'd been diagnosed with cancer and everything had changed. "We're like a family here. The reason why Angel River is as special as it is, is because our particular way of doing things runs through every inch of our operation."

"From horses to hot tubs?"

She couldn't tell if he was mocking or not. "As a matter of fact, yes."

"She still might be of help," he said. "Sybil cut her teeth in a five-star resort in Switzerland."

"This is Wyoming," Rory reminded. "We're a long way from Switzerland."

"With the prices you charge, not so much."

Her chin went up. "You think we're overpriced?"

"I didn't say that." His voice was mild, but that didn't stop her from being defensive. "What I am saying," he continued, "is that you have some key positions that have needed filling for too long. Particularly when you're trying to maintain a certain level of service. Sybil might be able to help you with one of them." He pulled a small leather case from his back pocket. He flipped it open and removed a business card that he set on her counter next to her clenched fingers. "That's her number." He returned the case to his pocket.

Rory wished she didn't notice the way his movements stretched his expensively casual gray sweater across his chest. "Is that why you walked up here? Just to give me Sybil's contact information?"

He frowned slightly. "Actually, I came up here because it's a nice walk and if I'd spent another minute with my brother, somebody would've been fishing him out of the river where I wanted to throw him."

Her jaw dropped.

"And I wish I were exaggerating," he said grimly.

Then he turned on his heel and left the kitchen. "I'm sorry I stepped on your candy, Killy," she heard him say a moment before she heard the front door open and close.

Rory's shoulders slumped.

She pressed her hand to the fluttering in her

chest, then dashed through the living room and followed him out the door.

Gage's stride was something to behold. She had to jog to catch up to him. When she did, she stared at the unlit cigarette he'd tucked in the corner of his mouth. "I didn't know you smoked."

He gave her an irritated look and palmed the cigarette, returning it to the battered pack he pulled from his jacket. "I don't."

She raised her eyebrows. "Looks are deceiving, I guess."

He exhaled and gazed behind her at the cluster of staff cabins that comprised Angel Camp, probably wishing she'd return to hers. "I quit smoking years ago. I carry the pack because—" He exhaled softly and shook his head, pocketing the pack again. "I don't know why," he muttered.

"My ex-husband was a recovering alcoholic," she admitted. "He kept a full bottle of whiskey on the shelf. Like a reminder. But if he was feeling stressed about something, he'd take it off the shelf. Set it on the table and just stare at it."

"Is that why you split up? Because he drank?"

"We split up because he was a liar and a cheat," she said evenly. "But actually, to be fair, Jon never did fall off the wagon. Not while we were together, at least, no matter how many times he took that bottle down. So maybe in his case, the method worked."

"Maybe he stayed sober for you and his son."

She couldn't help the derisive snort. "Jon's never even met Killy."

"Never?" Gage's expression made her wish she'd controlled her wayward tongue.

She scuffed her boot sole against the gravel and shook her head. "Why were you frustrated with Noah today?"

"Because I'm always frustrated with him," Gage muttered. He slowly turned his head as if his neck were paining him. "He's lazy. Moody and spoiled. Kid has never appreciated everything he has going for him."

"Sounds like a teenager."

"Which he isn't."

"Obviously you know him best, but he certainly admires you."

It was Gage's turn to snort. "He can't stand the air I breathe." He started to reach into his pocket again but checked the motion. "Which he told me in no uncertain terms earlier today."

"Why?"

He spread his hands. "Imagine any reason under the sun," he said. "There's a good chance he's thought of it and blames me for it."

"Like bringing him here in the first place?" Gage had told her Noah's choice had been Gage or jail, but she found that a little hard to believe. "Is he feeling too cooped up here at the ranch?"

"It's what I expected, but—" He shook his head. "He's very taken with you," he said abruptly.

She gave a half laugh. "Please. Marni's a much more likely object of his attention. She's the one who has a crush on him. I'm just a…a big sister figure or someth—"

Gage touched her lips with his finger, shocking her into silence. "There are a lot of things I don't know about my brother." His voice was low. "But this isn't one of them."

His hand dropped away immediately, but the damage was done. She could hardly think past the tingling in her lips. She took a step away, clearing her throat. "You don't have to worry," she finally managed in an only slightly garbled tone. "We discourage our crew from having personal relationships with guests."

He looked skeptical. "And the rule applies to you?"

The memory of him overhearing her conversation with Megan was much too fresh. "Yes." Her tone grew firmer. "Even me." *Especially me.*

"Is it worth someone's job if they violate the policy?"

"You mean would we fire someone over it?"

"You're a family here," he reminded her. "You going to fire one of your 'family' for getting too cozy with a guest?"

Now she was certain he was mocking her. The way he'd air-quoted the word *family* clinched it, and it set her teeth on edge.

"If I had to," she said flatly. "Maybe you can't

prevent those lines from being crossed in a company as large as yours, but here?" She crossed her arms over her chest. "You needn't worry about your brother where I'm concerned. Or Marni or Megan or anyone else, for that matter. I can promise you that your little brother is perfectly safe from all of us."

"I'm more worried that all of you aren't perfectly safe from him."

That took the wind out of her sails for a moment. "Marni can handle herself."

"Oh, for Go—" He broke off, swallowing his obvious impatience. "Not Marni. *You.*"

She tossed out her arms, exasperated as well. "What on earth for? I just told you I don't get involved with guests!"

He closed the distance she'd put between them. "Noah has a way of getting under people's skin."

"Well, not mine," she quickly assured him. The only one getting under her skin was Gage, and she had no intention of admitting it.

The only question was how long she'd be able to hide it.

Chapter Seven

Despite Rory's anxiety, the following days slid into a fairly easy routine.

Gage mucked stalls several times—with and without her. She showed him the compost setup and drove him over to Seth's place to introduce them. She'd been surprised by the knowledge Gage had when it came to the vagaries of cattle ranching. But by then, she ought to have known better where he was concerned. The man really did seem to know something about most everything. By the end of the week, he'd spent as much time with Seth as he had with her.

She knew Gage had seen plenty of her father, too, because half the time when she returned with Killy from the bus stop, she found them together in the office. The day before, in fact, they'd been playing chess.

She hadn't seen her dad play since before her mother died.

She'd crept back out of the office, leaving them to it, and spent a few extra hours with her son, which was never a bad thing.

She rarely saw Noah, though. Even though she'd joked about putting him down for the daylong ride that weekend, she hadn't. Nor had he added his name to the list, which settled Gage's claim that Noah was "taken with" her as far as she was concerned. According to Marni, Noah emerged daily when Frannie got there to clean the cabin, usually walking down to the river.

Always alone.

Rory considered asking Gage if Noah would be better off with his own cabin—they had plenty available, and maybe it would be less stressful for the brothers if they had more space between them. But she decided against sticking her nose where it didn't belong. If Gage had thought that arrangement would be better, it would already be a done deal.

In fact, after their last conversation about Noah, Gage had barely mentioned his name to her again. She hoped that meant they had reached some sort of détente, but she had her doubts.

Gage didn't offer any more staffing suggestions, either, and she was glad. She posted the spa manager position again on a few more websites and even scheduled a phone interview with a possible office assistant.

But when the candidate didn't bother to answer the phone at their agreed-upon time—or even bother to return the message Rory had left—she'd tossed the girl's application in the trash. It briefly made her wonder if she should have accepted Gage's help. But only briefly.

Regrettably, Gage still gave her that shiver down her spine whenever he was around. But at least by the end of the week she'd more or less regained her ability to keep her train of thought whenever their gazes happened to meet.

Though she'd succeeded on that score, her dreams at night were still rife with him. She'd gotten so she was afraid to go to sleep for fear that she'd be blushing the next day when she had to face him again.

Of course, Megan thought the entire situation was hilarious when Rory admitted the problem and tried to get out of the long trail ride she'd committed to before Gage and his brother had even arrived at the ranch.

"No way, girlfriend." Megan was using a curry brush on Moonbeam and didn't miss a stroke as she gave Rory a look. "Willow is signed up and if I have to listen to her exclaim over every little thing for hours on end, so do you. This was your idea, if you recall. So you're going. You're just getting the heebie-jeebies because Gorgeous Gage will be there. Besides. You want to disappoint Killy? This is the first time you're letting him go out with us."

Knowing that Megan was right didn't help. Feeling entirely out of sorts, Rory returned to the lodge. The sight of Gage pacing back and forth on the deck outside the great room while he talked on the phone was now commonplace.

She supposed a man like him couldn't get away from his business demands for long. Even Tig—who rarely spent less than a month at a time at Angel River—had to check in occasionally, and it was his wife who actually ran their business.

Two new bookings had arrived that week—the Murphys and the Delgados—and she stopped long enough to check in on them where they were sitting near the fireplace before heading back to her office.

She paid some bills and made some calls, including one confirming the officiant she'd arranged for the upcoming wedding. She was doodling on her desk pad while she listened to yet another voice mail from Bitsy Pith—the mother of the bride—when Gage entered the office. His gaze skated over her face and she pretended to give the voice mail more attention than it actually warranted. Before long his cell phone rang and he left again.

She hung up while Bitsy's message was still playing. So far, in the half dozen that the woman left, she'd changed her mind over the welcome reception menu every single time. Now she was back to the one she'd originally chosen four months ago.

Rory made yet another note for Chef Bart to add to his increasingly thick pile and left the office to pick up Killy. She was just pulling away from the lodge in the utility vehicle when she noticed Noah sitting on the front porch of his cabin.

She didn't have a lot of patience with someone who was guilty of driving under the influence, but there was still something about the young man that tugged at her. No matter what Gage said about his brother, she recognized unhappiness when she saw it and felt sympathy.

She pulled the UTV around to stop in front of his cabin and sent him a smile. "Hey there, stranger. Want to go for a spin?"

His hair was in a messy twist on his head, and he needed a shave. With the slouchy athletic pants and shapeless sweatshirt that hung on his thin frame, he definitely looked the part of the lazy brother. But he pushed off his chair and climbed in. "Where to?"

"Nowhere exciting. The bus stop. I need to pick up my son after school." When he didn't make any attempt to climb back out, she started off again. "Frannie cleaning?"

He nodded.

"Hear you've been exploring down by the river. You know that's the route we'll be taking on the ride tomorrow. We'll follow it all the way around to Overlook Camp. Those are the cabins I pointed out the day we rode up to the lookout. The leaves are about at their peak. It should be a beautiful ride."

She gave him a coaxing smile. "You really should come along. It'll be fun. Chef Bart sends us off with boxed lunches."

He gave a half laugh. "Is that supposed to be a real perk?"

"Some people think so." She grinned. "My son does, at any rate."

"Killy, right?"

"Yep. He's six. Nearly everything is an adventure where he's concerned. It'll be his first time going on a long ride with us. Usually he spends the day with my father or his friend Damon. Frannie's boy." She slowed to take the fork in the loop road. "This time they're both coming."

"Who else?"

She wondered if that was his way of finding out if his brother was going. "Most everyone here. We don't have any new guests arriving for a while." Not until the wedding group was due the following weekend.

"You don't have a lot of business, do you?"

"Ouch." She gave him a pointed look. "I'm surprised you noticed, considering you barely stick your nose out of the cabin."

His lips twitched. "Ouch," he returned.

The first day they'd arrived, she hadn't thought there was much resemblance between him and Gage, but times like this had her rethinking. "We don't have as much business as we usually do this time of year," she admitted. "But I'm working on it."

"Is that what Gage is doing with you?"

She gave him another look, longer this time. "Do the two of you *ever* talk?"

"Not if we can help it."

That was inconceivable to her. "He's learning how we do what we do."

"Why?"

There didn't seem to be any point in hiding it. "So he can turn around and do it better with his own guest ranch." They were jostled as they drove over bumps in the road.

"That's Gage. Always has to be better than everyone else."

She didn't see it. Not after the past week. Yes, he collected information and knowledge like some people collected coins, but when it came down to it, he was a lot less arrogant than she'd expected.

It still didn't mean she trusted him.

They arrived at the stop just as the big yellow bus was pulling up. Toonie came off first, not looking up from her paperback as she headed to her dad's pickup. The boys were next, throwing the usual football. But this time, when it went sailing over Killy's head, Noah leaped out of the utility vehicle and caught it neatly.

It was the fastest she'd seen him move, so she probably had the same look of astonishment on her face as her son did. Noah flipped the ball expertly to her son, and this time Killy did catch it. Astrid was yelling for Damon to hurry up, so the boys waved at each other and Killy jogged over to the UTV.

He peered up at Noah. "Are you my mom's boyfriend?"

Rory gaped. "Killy! Of course he isn't."

Noah just laughed.

"Noah's staying in one of the guest cabins." She gestured for Killy to climb into the narrow wedge of a rear seat. "Use the seat belt."

He did as told, but hung forward as she turned the vehicle around to leave. "Are you a football player?"

Noah laughed again. Which had to be a record for number of times that happened in a day. "No. Are you?"

Killy grinned broadly. His skinny chest puffed out beneath his jacket. "I will be."

"It's good to have goals," Noah told him.

"Yes, it is." Rory caught his eye. "So. About the ride tomorrow?"

He looked from Killy back to her again. "Yeah, fine. I mean, who can resist a boxed lunch?"

Turned out, no one got a boxed lunch after all.

Because the next morning, they woke to a torrential downpour that lasted the entire day.

"If I didn't know better, I'd think you did some fancy rain dance to conjure this up," Megan said as she and Rory stood together in the lodge staring out the window over the deck. "But as much as I know you wanted to avoid another full-on day with the

Gorgeous G, not even you have the skill for this."
Outside, the rain was coming down in sheets.

Behind them, the guests were all sprawled out
waiting for Bart to ring the dinner bell. The rainy
day had turned them into happy couch potatoes.
Even Willow was quiet for once, her legs over Tig's
lap while he read a book.

The only ones missing were Noah and Gage.
She'd seen Gage for a while earlier; he'd been talking to Willow and the Delgados. But then he'd disappeared.

She doubted that he was happily couch potato-
ing along with his brother in the Brown cabin. More
likely, he was off somewhere talking on his phone.

Killy and Damon, on the other hand, were practically bouncing off the walls after being cooped
inside all day long. Right now, they were running
up and down the hallway near the office. "I need to
get these guys out of here," she told Megan. "You
and Marni okay holding down the fort with Bart?"

"Have we ever *not* been okay?" Megan's brows
rose meaningfully. "I'm gonna set up the white
screen in here while they're having dinner, and we'll
watch Humphrey and Ingrid stare longingly at each
other while we make s'mores in the fireplace. It'll
be one of those unexpected nights that guests go
home raving about."

So Rory corralled the boys and tucked them into
her pickup to drive them back up to Angel Camp.
She stopped off in front of her dad's cabin to see if

he wanted to come up to their place to share the pan of lasagna she'd stolen from Bart. Leaving the boys in the truck, she darted through his front door. "I've got food—" She broke off.

Her dad was sitting at his table eating pizza with Gage, and both of them gave her a surprised look. "Everything all right, honey?" her dad asked.

She knew her jaw was flapping in the breeze. She nodded. "Just, uh, just checking that you—" she bumped into the door as she backed her way out "—you got dinner okay. Gottheboys. Gottarun." She slammed the door on her way out and ran back to the truck.

Rain was dripping from her hair into her eyes when she slid behind the wheel again.

"Thought we was getting Grandpa," Killy said.

"We *were*," she corrected absently as she drove the rest of the way to their cabin.

Chess. Pizza.

What else was going on that she didn't know about?

She got the boys inside, fed and eventually settled for the night in sleeping bags on the floor in Killy's room. She could still hear them giggling and whispering an hour later, but she didn't have the heart to come down on them. It meant that getting them going would be harder than ever the next morning, but since it wasn't the week she helped Bart make bread, it didn't matter.

She decided to draw herself a rare bath, then

poured a glass of wine and sank up to her neck in bubbles.

It was a small amount of bliss.

Which naturally meant it didn't have a chance in Hades of lasting.

She hadn't even gotten to the bottom of the wine-glass when she heard knocking on the door.

Somehow she knew it wasn't just anyone. Because everyone else would have just picked up the phone and called her. Gage was the only one to show up unexpectedly at her cabin time and time again.

She stood and sluiced away the bubbles before stepping out of the tub and pulling on her ancient bathrobe.

She tugged Killy's door the rest of the way closed as she passed his room and hurried downstairs. But by the time she reached the door, the knocking had stopped.

She opened it and stuck her head out. "Gage?"

He was just stepping down the porch steps and he turned. Not even he could act oblivious to the rain pouring down over the umbrella bearing the small Angel River logo. He had to have gotten the umbrella from her dad. The gift shop had run out of them months ago, and she hadn't yet reordered more.

She held her robe close to her throat. "Did you need something?" Even though most of her was tucked behind the doorway, he couldn't fail to notice she wasn't dressed for visitors.

"Sorry." He sounded oddly gruff. "Didn't mean

to interrupt your—" He broke off, gesturing. It seemed unlikely that he was as thrown by the sight of her as she'd been to find him eating pizza with her father, but for a gratifying moment, it felt that way.

"But you *are* here," she prompted. "And I can't help wondering why."

He took one of the porch steps. "Sean was telling me about the holiday season here."

Great. "What about it?"

"That it should be one of your busiest times, but this year it's not," he said bluntly. "Ever thought about offering a flash deal?"

She pushed her hair behind her ear, this time legitimately shivering from the cold and not his presence. "Done it, and we didn't even get a bump."

He moved up another step. "But did you do it for a holiday getaway? You know, most of your guests are coming here and staying a week or better. Tig—"

"Tig doesn't represent the majority of our guests."

"Fine. But my point is they're here for more than a couple nights. The Delgados? They're using all of their two weeks of vacation here."

"You think it's not a good thing for someone to *want* to spend an entire vacation here?"

"No, I'm saying it's expensive as hell." He raised a quick hand. "And I know Stanton resorts are expensive, too. But not a one of them is all-inclusive. It's a different animal entirely."

She wasn't convinced of that, but she grabbed her coat from its hook and swung it around her shoulders before opening the door a few inches more. "Okay. So?"

"So I'm saying there's also a whole market of people who don't have time to invest in a full-blown vacation. They just want a quick getaway. Two nights. Three nights. Christmas is on a Friday this year. People come in Christmas Eve. Stay until the day after Christmas. Or even two days after. Still have time to get back to work on Monday before they start celebrating New Year's."

She tilted her head. "You make your people come into the office between Christmas and New Year's, don't you."

He just gave her a look. He'd reached the top of the steps, and he lowered the umbrella to one side.

She sighed and pulled the door wide. "I'm freezing. You might as well come in." Still wearing the coat over her robe, she went over to the couch and curled in the corner, dragging an afghan over herself for good measure.

He left the umbrella outside and closed the door. He didn't really look away from her, but she was certain that he was taking in every detail of the cabin. At least it was a little more orderly than the last time he'd been there.

"How's Nelson?"

She glanced at the fishbowl on the dining room table. "Still swimming. Don't you think it's a little late to start promoting a deal for *this* Christmas?"

"In a perfect world. But nothing's perfect. Come

up with a new angle. Offer a flash deal—a little taste of Angel River at a price they can't resist in a short-stay package. And promote the hell out of it in places you don't ordinarily think about."

He wasn't bubbling over with Willow-level enthusiasm, but still it was enough to intrigue her. "Say we did it," she said cautiously. "What happens if we actually get a good response? I don't have the staff to—"

"Keep your staff focused on a few key areas. You're not getting people in the door for the full Angel River experience." He wasn't quite pacing, but he was moving around the room as he talked. Same way she'd seen him do so often when talking on his phone. "You don't have to offer eight different activities every day to keep them entertained. You're giving them a taste, remember?" He held up his hand. "Food, booze, ambience." He ticked them off. "You've got that covered without anyone having to step foot outside the lodge. Play up the season. All the feel-good stuff people fantasize about for the holidays." He stopped moving and closed his hands over the back of the couch beside her.

She looked away from those long, blunt-edged fingers. "You think that feel-good stuff is just a fantasy?" It was hard to even voice that particular word in his presence without feeling hot inside.

"I think people get caught up in the season and then reality hits."

"Well, hello, Mr. Scrooge," she murmured. "Is

this 'taste of'—" she air-quoted the words "—the sort of thing you have in mind for your ranch on Rambling Mountain?"

"Right now the only thing I have in mind for the Rad is a new name." He suddenly leaned forward on his arms, which brought his head almost down to her level. She couldn't help sucking in a silent breath and shrinking back against the cushions.

Fortunately, he didn't seem to notice. "Speaking of the name, I keep seeing the Angel River logo forged onto metal signs and things. Custom work, obviously. What company did you use?"

She managed to slide off the couch with something approaching casualness. "Nobody you want to work with."

"Why? Difficult to deal with?"

"Something like that." She clasped her arms in front of her. "My ex-husband did it for us."

Gage's eyes glinted with surprise. "When you said he'd never met Killy, for some reason I assumed he'd also never been here at all."

"It was before Killy," she said. "Jon was a guest here."

He straightened slowly. "Is that how you met?"

She wished she'd left off that detail. "I designed the logo, but he did the work." She'd been falling for him from that moment on.

"*You* designed the logo?"

"Don't look so shocked. I do have some skills besides mucking out horse stalls!"

His gaze seemed to look straight down inside her. "Never doubted it."

She was afraid that the shivers resulting from his innuendo would plague her for days.

Chapter Eight

She was right on that score.

In fact, even a week later, she was afraid they'd actually worsened. She felt like she was living on pins and needles where the man was concerned, and by the following Saturday, without Killy there to distract her because he was at Damon's, she resorted to desperate measures.

She got out a chain saw.

If shoveling horse manure couldn't relieve her tension, maybe cutting down the stump in her front yard would.

The torrential rain that postponed their trail ride had moved on after only a day, leaving in its wake a glorious week, weatherwise. The only downside was that the downpour had knocked all the fall leaves from the trees. Every time she looked down at the river, the bare, knobby branches reminded her of skeleton fingers. With everything looking so barren, she wanted the snow to come and soften the landscape whether it was good for Thanksgiving business or not.

She'd also had to spend a day polishing windows at the Uptown camp all over again after the storm. The wedding party was coming in the next day, and she wanted everything to be perfect.

The stump was a good four feet tall and half again as wide. Reducing it to smithereens would take time, even with the chain saw. She was counting on the task to do the trick of reducing her Gage nerves.

She circled the stump, feeling the bright sun on her bare head as she throttled the engine.

But as she eyed the thing, she suddenly saw potential in the dead wood.

She dropped her safety glasses down onto her nose and revved the engine on her chain saw again. The first dip she made against the stump sent a jolt right up through her shoulders.

After that, everything else fell away as she worked. First she made broad, rough swipes that cut away the excess wood from around the shape she saw within. Then she got a little more detailed. A little finer.

Gage heard the chain saw long before he realized that Rory was at the center of the sawdust arching out around her.

And then he couldn't do anything *but* watch, half his heart in his throat and his blood pooling hotly because of the way she swung the dangerous saw around.

It was like watching a dancer. She was so intent on what she was doing, she never even noticed him standing out of range of the spray of disintegrating wood. The saw whined as she angled an incision here, coaxed a curve there.

And then, suddenly, she was done.

She killed the engine and let the tip of the guide bar down at her side. She was breathing hard, her shoulders rising and falling from the exertion. And the expression on her face...

Euphoric.

He ran his hand around his neck, reminding himself that following the instinct to toss her over his shoulder and haul her back to his cave would be universally frowned upon.

She was circling the stump again. But it was no longer a stump at all, and her fingertips danced over the delicate-looking tip of the single unfurled wing that had taken its place. The graceful arc of wood could have been modeled after a peregrine, it was so vividly perfect. "When you talked about skills, you weren't joking."

She jerked around, obviously startled, and pulled off her safety glasses. "I didn't realize I'd gained an audience."

Her cheeks were flushed. Her eyes brilliant.

Everything about her radiated joy. "How could you, when you were playing with that toy?" He gestured toward the wicked-looking chain saw. "Remind me never to get you angry."

Expression sparkling, she set the saw on her patio along with the glasses and began swiping at the slivers of wood clinging to her sweater. It looked like a fairly hopeless endeavor to him, but his fingers still itched to lend aid.

"Are you here for a reason or just to make fun?"

"Not making fun," he assured her as he walked around the creation. "Have you always had a thing for wings?"

"Well, this *is* Angel River." Her smile was sexy as all hell.

"Where'd the name come from, though?"

She laughed outright. "The river, obviously. That's the name of it. Was the name of it before my dad bought this place and will be the name of it long after we're all gone." She leaned over to rake her fingers vigorously through her hair, releasing another cloud of sawdust before straightening and flipping it back.

He nearly swallowed his tongue.

"Now, back to the reason you're—" She broke off at the sight of Megan racing up the road in a UTV, waving her hand wildly.

The exuberance in Rory's expression drained away along with every speck of color in her face. "It always happens," she whispered. "Every time."

"Every time, what?" He slid his arm around her shoulder, because as strong and vibrant as she'd looked carving a falcon's wing out of an ugly tree stump, now she looked brittle enough to shatter to pieces.

But she didn't answer. She just waited until Megan's vehicle skidded to a stop a few feet away.

He saw the quick concern in the woman's eyes as she took in Rory's obvious alarm. "The Uptown group arrived."

Gage felt Rory sag before she suddenly spun away from him, racing inside her house and slamming the door shut after her.

"What the hell?" He glanced at Megan. "One minute she's—" he waved at the stunning bird wing "—and the next it's like she's seen a ghost."

Megan looked from the cabin to the sculpture, seeming to realize something. "Rory created that?"

"With a freaking chain saw. I've never seen—" He broke off. "I'm checking on her," he muttered.

"Be gentle," Megan called after him, entirely unlike her usual self. "Remember what I told you about Sean?"

It took him a minute to make the connection. Earlier that week, when the two of them had been cleaning the horse barn, she'd been recounting the days when Sean had run the place. She'd told him about the day he collapsed, seemingly out of the blue, leading to his cancer diagnosis. "What about it?"

"I was the one who found him."

"Yeah, you told me."

"And I was the one who came up here to tell Rory. She was in her studio working." She looked pointedly at the carving. "Something she hasn't done until now."

Every time. That's what Rory had whispered.

He realized it would have made a lot more sense for Rory's best friend to go in and check on her now, but he went inside the cabin instead. He found Rory in the downstairs bathroom, retching.

He swallowed an oath and slid in beside her— not sure what he could do, but only knowing he needed to do something. She swatted a hand at him, obviously thinking otherwise, and yanked down a towel that she pressed to her face as she flushed the toilet and sat back against the wall. "Go away." Her voice was muffled by the towel.

He wished he could. His life was complicated enough without this. The simple solution would have been to let Megan deal with this.

But he hadn't. And he knew he wouldn't.

So he ran another small towel under the faucet and nudged it into Rory's lax fingers.

Her shoulders moved with a heavy sigh and she exchanged the bath towel for the smaller one, pressing it to her face.

She seemed out of danger of needing the commode, and he lowered the lid to sit. "You're an artist."

Resignation filled her eyes above the edge of the wet towel.

"So why are you running Angel River?"

She swore suddenly and pushed to her feet, using his thighs as leverage in the small space. She stuck her mouth right beneath the sink tap, rinsed and spat, and hurried out of the bathroom.

He followed her back outside to where Megan was still sitting in the UTV.

"The wedding party's not due until tomorrow afternoon," Rory said as if she hadn't just taken a momentary detour.

Megan spread her hands. "Nevertheless, they *are* here. Seth heard they'd landed at the airstrip, and he and Marni shuttled them all to the lodge. Marni said she called you but you didn't answer." Her gaze slid briefly to the wing. "They just arrived." She took a bracing breath. "All fifty-four of them."

"Fifty-four!" Rory's voice rose with disbelief. Her color had returned, and she propped her hands on her hips. Wood splinters still littered the shoulders of her sweater. "Last week they confirmed thirty-six!"

"Gonna be a fun ten days," Megan predicted.

"Why?" Rory tilted back her head. "Hardly any business and now too much?" She had a newly determined look about her. "Uptown has the space, but we're talking eighteen extra people. Do we know if it's just a few extra families?"

"Marni was trying to work that out when I left. I saw some kids in the group, but as for the adults... I recognize a bunch of bar patrons when I see them."

She nodded sagely. "Mark my words, we're going to burn through some booze with this group."

"I'm not worried about the liquor supply. I'm worried about the workload." Rory rubbed her cheek, swiping at the fine sawdust clinging to her skin. "The bride's mom has told me more than once they'll want a babysitter. Call Astrid. Make sure she'll be available. Marni won't be able to do it now. We'll need her to run activities. Chef knows we've got extra heads?"

Megan nodded.

"All right, then." Rory looked like she was about to climb into the UTV. Then she flushed, dusting her hands off on her jeans. "I'll clean up first before heading down there." She raked her hair back from her face. "Can you help Marni in the lodge until I get there?"

Megan shook her head. "I have the afternoon ride in less than an hour. I don't even have the horses ready yet."

"I'll help at the lodge," Gage offered, and both women looked at him almost as if they'd forgotten he was there.

It was curiously refreshing. And surprisingly deflating. "I *can* mix a drink, at least."

"But—" Rory broke off whatever protest she was about to make. Obviously, she'd decided desperate times meant even his help was better than nothing. She tugged down the hem of her splinter-ridden sweater, her eyes skipping away from his. "I appreciate it."

Then she gestured at the utility vehicle. "Megan can take you down to the lodge before she gets going on the ride." She didn't wait for his agreement but headed straight back to her cabin, scooping up the chain saw along the way.

Gage sat down beside Megan in the UTV, his attention still on Rory's departing form. "How much time did she spend in her studio before Sean got sick?"

Megan hit the gas and pulled out of the drive, aiming down the hill toward the main camp. "All of it. I know that was just a knee-jerk reaction back there, but after this long, you'd think—" She broke off and shook her head. "Losing her mom was bad enough. I was the one who called her about that, too."

"What happened?"

Megan glanced at him. "She died on the rapids."

Rory's sad eyes the day they'd been up on the lookout finally made sense to him.

"Rory and Jon hadn't even been married a year when it happened. They'd just moved to Seattle."

He had a hard time envisioning Rory anywhere other than Angel River. "She told me he's the one who did the ironwork with the logo."

Megan's eyebrows rose. "She usually acts like he never existed."

"And that he was a liar and a cheat."

That earned him another surprised look. "He

was. And he walked out on her right after she discovered she was pregnant with Killy. Miserable worm," she added under her breath.

It didn't take a math whiz to realize her marriage had lasted about as long as his. Or that it had ended shortly after her mother died. "She came back here after that."

"Yeah. Her folks built the studio before she went to art school. She used to make a ton of stuff that got sold in the gift shop. When she came back after Jon, she didn't go in the studio much. After Killy was born, she got back to it. Like she'd found the joy again because of him. But once Sean got sick, she closed the door and stepped in as manager."

He knew that much from Sean. Knew too that the awards from travel magazines had come less often. That the occupancy rates had been on a slow decline. It wasn't that Rory wasn't good at running the guest ranch.

But the problem was plain as day to him now that he'd seen her artistry. Rory might love the guest ranch. But her heart wasn't in it the way it was in her art.

As if she'd been reading his mind, Megan shook her head. "I still can't believe she carved that wing." She whipped around the fork, aiming for the main camp.

He could hardly believe it, either, and he'd watched the live performance. "Drop me at the Brown cabin. I'll walk across to the lodge."

She spun the wheel again, and gravel spit from the tires as they slid to a stop in front of his cabin. He stepped out and had barely cleared the front bumper when the wrangler took off again.

He noted the two shuttle buses parked in front the lodge as he quickly went inside. Noah was still sprawled on the couch in the exact position he'd been occupying earlier.

"Get up," Gage ordered, shoving his brother's bare feet off the coffee table. "Put on clean clothes. Time you started earning your keep."

Looking bored, Noah lifted his middle finger.

Gage ignored it. "Rory needs help."

"So?" Despite Noah's insolent tone, his hand dropped.

Gage pulled off his jacket and started up the stairs. He wanted a clean shirt. "That wedding group she's been expecting came a day early and with a lot of unexpected plus-ones." He pulled off his sweater and looked over his shoulder.

Noah was sitting straighter on the couch, though he still hadn't made any effort to stand.

Gage continued up the stairs. "You and I," he said over the banister, "are going to do whatever we need to do to help her out."

"Like what?"

Gage entered his bedroom and pulled a clean white shirt from the closet. As he buttoned it up, he grimaced at his reflection in the mirror on the back of the door. Noah wasn't the only one who needed a shave.

He headed back downstairs, shoving his shirt-tails into his jeans. "Bartending, for one thing," he told Noah, picking up where he'd left off. He knew it would get his brother's attention even more than mentioning Rory had.

Noah's head lifted. In the weeks they'd been there, his blue eyes had finally lost their bloodshot tinge. They were clearer than Gage could remember them being in a long, long while. Even after the last stint in rehab.

"That doesn't mean you get to imbibe. And if I see you try, I'll kick your butt from here to Denver," he warned. "And I'm assuming you know how to actually mix a cocktail without having someone do it for you."

Noah sneered as he unfurled himself from the couch. "Better mixologist than you'll ever be." He bounded up the stairs with more energy than he'd shown in years.

This huge inconvenience for Rory and Angel River was so far proving to be the best thing that had happened to Gage in dealing with the Noah problem.

He scrubbed his hand down his jaw, thinking about shaving again, but his cell phone interrupted the thought. Seeing the name on the display, he briefly considered ignoring it. He spoke with Archer routinely, hoping for a resolution about Rambling

Mountain, and they were still in limbo. He swiped the screen. "Tell me something good, Archer."

"Nell's having a boy."

Gage forgot about business and smiled broadly. "No kidding? Congratulations!" He pulled on his jacket again and went out onto the porch. Over at the lodge, a trio of women was dancing on the deck outside the great room. Their laughter carried easily. "When're you going to get her down the aisle?" The two had been engaged for a few months now.

"Before the year is over," Archer said. "I told Nell I wasn't waiting any longer. She should be getting past the morning sickness sometime soon. It's not as though we're planning some huge, formal wedding. We just want our family and friends there. That includes you, in case you're entertaining some notion of hiding out at Angel River to get out of being my best man."

Family and friends.

Gage rubbed his forehead, feeling a sudden headache coming on. He should never have agreed to be Archer's best man. It was getting too complicated.

"My grandmother's already offered up her mansion for the I dos," Archer continued. "Since Nell started working for Vivian this summer, they've gotten pretty close. We'll probably take her up on it."

Which meant Gage definitely needed to get out of being best man. He'd avoided meeting Vivian Templeton in person for several years now.

He looked over his shoulder into the cabin, holding his phone away from his mouth. "Noah," he yelled. "Get the lead out." The noise from the lodge was growing louder. At the rate Noah was going, Rory would beat them there.

Gage put the phone back to his ear. "Sorry about that."

"How's everyone's favorite little brother doing?"

"If he's not ignoring me, he's telling me to go to hell." Or worse. "But he's sober. Been that way since we got here."

"And you're what? Halfway through the stay?"

"Nearly." It felt like a small eternity even to him, and he wasn't plagued by the same demons that his brother was.

"Learning anything important about running a guest ranch?"

"Yeah." Gage eyed the group at the lodge. Despite the temperature hovering somewhere in the mid-forties, one of the girls was dancing around in a bikini, and someone was tossing confetti over the side of the deck. "You gotta know how to manage manure."

Rory felt the pulse of music from the lodge even before she entered through the storeroom.

Bart was working in the kitchen, prepping a mountain of vegetables. He wore a pair of noise-canceling headphones and gave her a benign smile as she passed through. She was pretty sure nothing ever knocked him off his even keel. Not even eighteen extra mouths to feed.

In the great room, the music was almost deafening. She glanced at all the unfamiliar faces and was glad that the guests they'd welcomed that week—the Jorgensons, Lilys and Mattas had replaced the Delgados and Murphys—were out on the afternoon ride with Megan. Tig and Willow were gone, too, spending the afternoon at the spa with Donna.

Megan had said the arrivals totaled fifty-four, but as Rory sidled through the crowd, it felt like twice that many. Which just reminded her how long it had been since they'd had such a full house at Angel River.

She spotted Marni's pink hair and angled toward her.

The young woman was gamely trying to deal with an angry, red-faced man. "Missy, I've paid good money to—"

Rory stopped next to him, her hand extended. "Good afternoon," she said loud enough to be heard above the music. "I'm Rory McAdams, manager here at Angel River. You must be Mr. Pith." Before he had a chance to transfer his baleful look to her, she took his clammy hand and pumped it enthusiastically. "How was your flight from Florida?"

"Bumpy," he complained.

"Landing at the airstrip often is," she said with a nod. "Has something to do with the mountains. Is Mrs. Pith here?"

"She's off with Sabrina somewhere," he said dismissively. Sabrina was the bride. "She's not real pleased the welcome spread we expected is nowhere to be found."

Rory kept her smile in place. The "welcome spread" would have been quite in place if his party had arrived on the right day. "Perhaps we could go to the office for a few minutes," she suggested. "Finalize some details."

"Bitsy said everything was all set." He looked irritated, the lines on his bulbous nose turning even bluer. "What's there to finalize?"

She leaned closer so she didn't have to yell to be heard. "She confirmed your group for a few less people than you actually have, so we need to review the rooms and cabins you'll need." She wasn't mentioning their early arrival until she knew that *she* hadn't made the error. "My office is just this way." She extended her arm and, since she was still clasping his hand, managed to get him to take a few steps in the right direction.

Fortunately, once he'd started moving, it was easy enough to keep him moving.

They were nearly out of the great room when she spotted Gage and Noah standing behind the mahogany bar. They were both wearing white shirts rolled up at the elbows and tucked into their jeans. Noah's long hair was tied up in a man bun. Gage's shorter hair was tumbling over his forehead.

They both had cocktail shakers in their hands, and a row of young women—she'd bet her goldfish that they were bridesmaids—was lined up in front of them.

More striking than anything, though, were both men's huge smiles.

It was enough to make *her* want to line up in front of them, too.

"Are we going to your office or not?"

She hadn't realized she'd slowed. She quickly looked away from Gage.

He's a guest. Only that particular line was getting blurry right now.

"Yes, Mr. Pith." She let go of the man's beefy hand and briskly led the way. When they reached the office, she invited him to sit in the living area. "Can I get you something to drink?"

"Coffee," he muttered.

She was relieved it wasn't a cocktail.

She flipped on the coffee maker behind the desk and stuck in a pod, leaving it to heat while she pulled out the reservation book and the Pith file. She distinctly remembered that Bitsy Pith had sent a fax with the original dates of the registration, and Rory flipped through the file until she found it.

She relaxed slightly when she had confirmation that the arrival date error was on the Piths' side. She found it much easier to be accommodating when she knew she wasn't in the wrong.

When the coffee was done brewing, she carried the cup and the reservation book into the living area. "Do you take sugar or cream?"

He shook his head. "Whiskey."

Probably explained the state of his nose. She set the coffee in front of him and pulled a bottle of whiskey she kept for just such occasions from the desk drawer.

She added a measure to his cup and then sat beside him, opening up the book. "These are the room configurations at Uptown Camp," she told him as she unfolded an oversize diagram.

"We're not in the lodge here?"

She couldn't help but wonder how much conversation went on between Bitsy and Bobby Pith. "The Uptown Camp is a private setting for you and your guests," she explained, pulling out the brochure containing the map of the entire Angel River valley. She pointed out the collection of cabins with her pencil. "It's an easy ride from here to there." She pretended not to see the face he made and returned her attention to the Uptown reservation chart that contained head counts for each cabin.

She also used the chart to keep track of everyone's individual welcome totes, which she hadn't put together yet because they'd arrived a day early. "If you can let me know the additional number of rooms or cabins that you need, I can—"

"We don't need any additional anything. We're already paying you a living fortune for this wedding business."

Her fingers tightened on her pencil. The inclusive wedding package the Piths had chosen had a built-in discount, which even at the original count amounted to a considerable sum. She was willing to negotiate the extra cost of the unexpected guests to smooth over the situation, but she wasn't going to accommodate them for free. "Mr. Pith, just the other day, your wife confirmed your final number of guests at thirty-six."

"So?"

"You arrived with more than fifty," she said, making an effort to keep her tone gentle.

"It's all the kids," he said with a dismissive flick of his fingers.

"And we're happy to have them," she assured him, swallowing another spurt of annoyance. "We pride ourselves on being family-friendly. We can configure all of our cabins to accommodate more children per room. The Homestead lodge in particular has a wing that can even be fashioned into a bunkhouse if all of the kids would like to sleep together, for instance." She smiled. "I have a six-year-old myself."

He gulped his hot, spiked coffee, seemingly undeterred by the steam coming off it. "You need to work this out with Bitsy."

She wanted to gnash her teeth. Instead, she rose immediately, tucking the book under her arm. "Certainly." Considering the state of things already, she'd be reviewing every single detail the woman *had* confirmed for the coming ten days, including the reception menu that Bart was working on.

Rory didn't want the entire ranch thrown into chaos for one minute longer than necessary.

"Let's go find her and get things sorted, and we can begin transporting luggage while you and your guests continue enjoying the lodge here. There's a bonfire near the river after dinner. It's always a lot of fun."

With a harrumph, Mr. Pith stood, too, and followed her out of the office.

He took the whiskey bottle with him.

Some guests were a positive joy. She was already certain that was not going to be the case where the Piths were concerned.

When they reentered the great room, it was slightly less crowded than it had been before. Her attention swerved to the bar.

Gage and his brother were both still working behind it, smiles on their faces.

With the bevy of bridesmaids still watching them raptly.

Maybe the Pith party hadn't stepped off on the most ideal footing. But if it kept a smile on the faces of Gage Stanton and his brother while they actually *worked* together, she had to admit that maybe, just maybe, it might all be worth it.

Chapter Nine

The lodge was finally empty when Rory reentered her office later that evening and closed the door.

At the sight of the white stationer boxes sitting on her desk, she let out a deep sigh. They contained the monogrammed paper that Bitsy expected to be used for anything relating to her daughter's wedding. Using special paper wouldn't be so bad. But there were ribbons to be added. Elaborately printed folders to be folded and filled with every manner of information for their guests.

And Bitsy expected Angel River to take care of it all.

At least Bart had told her that the dinner hour went well. While Rory had been here in the office trying to rearrange several months of effort in a single afternoon, the chef—not surprisingly—had more than risen to the occasion of feeding everyone.

Now, all the guests were down at the river for the bonfire, which left her time to finish the welcome totes and get them delivered to Uptown before they turned in for the night. Megan was coming by later to help.

She wearily pushed away from the door, popped a fresh pod in the coffee maker and rearranged the boxes that she'd stacked there earlier.

Then she pulled out the chart she'd redone and set to work. She was on her third cup of coffee and coaxing a piece of the fussy, deckled paper through her reluctant printer when the office door opened a few hours later.

"I hate this printer. And this paper—" she snatched up one of the ruined sheets from the floor and spun around in her desk chair "—is not help—" She broke off at the sight of Gage. Her grip tightened, wrinkling the paper even more. "I thought you were Megan."

He spread his hands slightly. "Not quite."

Her stomach suddenly felt jittery. She realized she was still clutching the paper and pitched it into the overflowing trash can beside the desk.

Behind her, the printer on the credenza clicked ominously, followed by the sound of paper crumpling. Again.

She sighed and grabbed her coffee mug, looking at Gage over the top of it. "Thought you were down at the bonfire." She'd seen him heading that way along with Tig and Willow.

"I was." He unzipped his leather jacket as he approached the desk. His gaze took in the mess of papers. "What's all that?"

She plucked one of her successes from the woefully small pile of them. "Next week's activity schedule."

"And those?" He nodded to the second stack of folded items sitting on the corner of her desk.

"Next week's activity schedule for anyone *not* involved with the Pith wedding." She sipped her coffee again. It was already lukewarm. "Thank you for your help before. Tell Noah how much I appreciate it. The extra hands really helped." She dragged her eyes away from the perfect fit of Gage's shirt against his chest. "You and Noah seemed to be quite the popular duo with the ladies."

He shrugged off her words and picked up one of the schedules. "What's the difference between the two? Their options are the same as everyone else staying here."

She set aside her mug. "Yes, but Bitsy Pith—" just saying the name annoyed her "—insists that for *her* guests, everything must match the wedding decor. Even our ordinary old activity schedule." She pointed her finger at him. "And get that expression off your face," she warned. "When it comes to weddings, you can expect all *sorts* of demands like this." She flicked one of the white boxes with her fingertip. "Wedding programs. Reception programs. Brunch programs. You name it and I'll bet you that Bitsy Pith has planned for it."

"Just because a demand is made doesn't mean it has to be met."

"It does when we're talking this much money," she muttered and spun around in her chair again to face the printer. She began freeing the jammed paper. "Is Noah at the bonfire?"

"He was when I left. First time he's actually gone down for one."

"When the two of you were serving drinks, he looked like he was enjoying himself. You both did." She glanced over her shoulder. He'd tossed his jacket on the couch, as if he planned to stay. She moistened her lips and quickly turned back to her printer. "It was a nice sight." She pulled harder on the paper and swallowed an oath when it began to tear.

"Did you even break for dinner?"

"No time." She flipped open a panel on the printer and pulled out the cartridge to work on the jammed paper from the inside. "I want to get the welcome totes over to Uptown before the bonfire breaks up." Which, considering her luck right now, could be any time. "The fire *is* still going strong, isn't it?"

He nodded. "Their group wasn't supposed to be here until tomorrow. Can't the totes wait until then?"

"Mrs. Pith—" she nearly spit the name "—doesn't understand that her group arrived a day early."

"Then she's a twit."

Rory couldn't help feeling a rush of gratitude at his words. "That's entirely possible. She didn't even have the actual ceremony date right in her paperwork. It's on Saturday instead of Sunday. Makes a person wonder what the wedding invitations were like, doesn't it?" Getting the date corrected wasn't as simple as just fixing the ranch calendar. It also meant Rory rearranging the officiant from Wymon. The flowers. The musicians. The bartenders and waitstaff she'd hired from town. Everything had needed to be moved forward a day.

"What about her husband?"

"Mr. Pith believes Mrs. Pith has everything organized like a top. And even though she most certainly does not, they're the clients, and our clients are never wrong."

"Even when they are."

"And particularly when they've written a big fat check," Megan said, walking into the office. She'd obviously overheard. When she spotted Rory's mess, her eyebrows rose. "Having fun?"

Rory ought to be grateful for Megan's arrival. "A blast. Exactly how I like spending my Saturday nights."

Gage had wandered closer and was watching the printer. "What do you usually do on Saturday nights?"

Megan laughed. "Rory? She hits the hay early, because she's in the kitchen with Bart making bread at the butt crack of dawn on Sunday mornings."

"Dawn would be too late," Rory murmured. She'd finally succeeded in working the ragged strip of paper free, and she replaced the cartridge and closed the panel. "And it's not every Sunday."

The printer whirred and clicked, warming up again. It was hard ignoring Gage standing so near, and she was grateful that her hand didn't shake when she reached for a fresh piece of paper. "Did you get the luggage over to Uptown?"

"Left it all in Homestead just where you told me," Megan said. "I'm surprised you didn't want it delivered to everyone's individual rooms like usual."

"If they hadn't come in a day early, I would have," Rory muttered. Maybe it was petty of her not to provide that particular convenience, but she chose to think of it as expedient.

"Pretty hoity-toity." Megan plucked a piece of marbled blue paper from an open box and ran her fingertip along the thin, rough edge. "This the part causing the problem?"

"I don't know if it's the deckled edge or the raised monogram." Rory held the paper lightly until the feeder finally gained traction, then didn't dare breathe while the sheet disappeared inside. A moment later, it emerged and settled lightly on the exit tray. "Hallelujah." She pulled it off the tray and folded it carefully.

She was painfully aware of Gage watching the whole process. She wasn't sure she'd ever felt quite so inept, and she really, *really* wished he'd stayed at the bonfire. So far, it'd been a banner day. First he saw her lose her lunch, and now this?

"These the directories?" Megan had transferred her attention to another stack of brochures with a map of Uptown and guest locations on one side and a map of the entire facility on the other.

Rory barely glanced her way as she turned to feed another sheet into the printer. "Yes."

It had taken her all afternoon to get the reservation mess straightened out and room keys distributed to the proper parties. The fact that Bitsy Pith was tipsy—and probably had been since before their private charter touched down in Wymon—hadn't helped, either. Keeping Bitsy focused on the matter at hand hadn't been easy.

Her husband's offhand dismissal of the additional guests as just being "kids" hadn't been remotely accurate, either.

Oh, yes, there were kids. Seven in all, but only two weren't in the original confirmation. The remaining additions to the party were adults.

"No wonder you said to just pile up all the luggage for them to sort out themselves."

"Yup." She held her breath again as the printer whirred softly. Rearranging the rooms and cabins had been easier than swallowing Bitsy's blame for the mix-up on the dates. Rory had proof that Bitsy was wrong, but she didn't argue. It had been more important that the woman had at least acknowledged they'd arrived with "a few" more people than

Get Up To 4 Free Books!

Dear Reader,

IT'S A FACT: if you answer 4 quick questions, we'll send you 4 FREE REWARDS from each series you try!

Try **Harlequin® Special Edition** books featuring comfort and strength in the support of loved ones and enjoying the journey no matter what life throws your way.

Try **Harlequin® Heartwarming™ Larger-Print** books featuring uplifting stories where the bonds of friendship, family and community unite.

Or **TRY BOTH!**

I'm not kidding you. As a leading publisher of women's fiction, we value your opinions… and your time. That's why we are prepared to reward you handsomely for completing our mini-survey. In fact, we have 4 Free Rewards for you, including 2 free books and 2 free gifts from each series you try!

Thank you for participating in our survey,

Pam Powers

To get your 4 FREE REWARDS:
Complete the survey below and return the insert today to receive up to 4 FREE BOOKS and FREE GIFTS guaranteed!

"4 for 4" MINI-SURVEY

1 Is reading one of your favorite hobbies?
☐ YES   ☐ NO

2 Do you prefer to read instead of watch TV?
☐ YES   ☐ NO

3 Do you read newspapers and magazines?
☐ YES   ☐ NO

4 Do you enjoy trying new book series with FREE BOOKS?
☐ YES   ☐ NO

Please send me my Free Rewards, consisting of **2 Free Books from each series I select** and **Free Mystery Gifts**. I understand that I am under no obligation to buy anything, as explained on the back of this card.

❏ **Harlequin® Special Edition** (235/335 HDL GQ4M)
❏ **Harlequin® Heartwarming™ Larger Print** (161/361 HDL GQ4M)
❏ **Try Both** (235/335 & 161/361 HDL GQ4X)

FIRST NAME   LAST NAME

ADDRESS

APT.#   CITY

STATE/PROV.   ZIP/POSTAL CODE

EMAIL ❏   Please check this box if you would like to receive newsletters and promotional emails from Harlequin Enterprises ULC and its affiliates. You can unsubscribe anytime.

SE/HW-820-MS20

HARLEQUIN READER SERVICE—Here's how it works:

Accepting your 2 free books and 2 free gifts (gifts valued at approximately $10.00 retail) places you under no obligation to buy anything. You may keep the books and gifts and return the shipping statement marked "cancel." If you do not cancel, approximately one month later we'll send you more books from the series you have chosen, and bill you at our low, subscribers-only discount price. Harlequin® Special Edition books consist of 6 books per month and cost $4.99 each in the U.S or $5.74 each in Canada, a savings of at least 17% off the cover price. Harlequin® Heartwarming™ Larger-Print books consist of 4 books per month and cost just $5.74 each in the U.S. or $6.24 each in Canada, a savings of at least 21% off the cover price. It's quite a bargain! Shipping and handling is just 50¢ per book in the U.S. and $1.25 per book in Canada*. You may return any shipment at our expense and cancel at any time — or you may continue to receive monthly shipments at our low, subscribers-only discount price plus shipping and handling. *Terms and prices subject to change without notice. Prices do not include sales taxes which will be charged (if applicable) based on your state or country of residence. Canadian residents will be charged applicable taxes. Offer not valid in Quebec. Books received may not be as shown. All orders subject to approval. Credit or debit balances in a customer's account(s) may be offset by any other outstanding balance owed by or to the customer. Please allow 3 to 4 weeks for delivery. Offer available while quantities last.

▲ If offer card is missing write to: Harlequin Reader Service, P.O. Box 1341, Buffalo, NY 14240-8531 or visit www.ReaderService.com ▲

BUSINESS REPLY MAIL
FIRST-CLASS MAIL   PERMIT NO. 717   BUFFALO, NY

POSTAGE WILL BE PAID BY ADDRESSEE

HARLEQUIN READER SERVICE
PO BOX 1341
BUFFALO NY 14240-8571

NO POSTAGE
NECESSARY
IF MAILED
IN THE
UNITED STATES

they'd intended and was willing to negotiate the additional cost.

Rory wasn't willing to chance the ill will from the people paying for an extravagant wedding over an incorrect date. Angel River needed good word of mouth. Good reviews.

"What's all this other stuff?" Megan didn't wait for an answer as she lifted one of the box lids.

"The rest of their custom printing. She expects us to assemble everything for them."

"Good grief." Megan pulled out a slim, engraved card and started reading. "'Sabrina Larissa Pith and Dante Cruz Castellano met on a cool spring evening—' oh, gag." She tossed the program back into the box. "I thought putting this stuff together was what bridesmaids were good for."

"Evidently, not in this case." The printer had managed to emit another page unscathed. Rory folded it and dropped it on the stack. But before she could add another sheet, Gage stepped in the way.

"Let me take a look at it."

"Printer maintenance another one of those things you've tried yourself?"

He gave her a sidelong glance, amusement in his eyes. "You'd be surprised at the things I'm capable of doing."

A flame flickered low inside her. At this point, she was pretty sure she *wouldn't* be surprised.

"How many more do you need to print?"

"Twenty." She didn't bother pointing out that

she'd already ruined more sheets than that. He could see her failures in the trash.

He suddenly crouched down in the narrow space between her and the credenza, and she couldn't help catching her breath.

He noticed. "Afraid I'll make things worse?"

Better for him to think she was worried about the stupid printer than to think it was his proximity making her nervous. "Maybe." She looked away, only to find Megan watching her with a knowing expression.

She turned back to Gage. He'd pulled open the panel, removed the cartridge and was feeling inside. "Have a small screwdriver? A piece is still jammed beneath that plate there. Here." He grabbed her hand and directed it into the printer cavity. "Feel."

Her pulse was suddenly pounding inside her head, and the only thing she felt was his fingers on hers. It was ridiculous. There was nothing intimate whatsoever about sticking one's hand inside an overworked desktop printer. Until Gage Stanton was involved.

"I feel it," she said quickly. A bald-faced lie that made even more heat rise to her cheeks. She tugged her hand free and bolted out of her chair. "I'll go find a screwdriver." She hurried out of the office, aware of the unholy glee in Megan's eyes as she followed.

"What'd I give you?" Megan asked in a loud whisper. "Three weeks?"

Rory slashed her hand in the air. "Shh!"

Megan's laugh wasn't even remotely muffled as they reached the empty great room. "You should have seen your face when he grabbed your hand. I thought your eyes were going to bug out of your head."

Rory glared at her. "Isn't there something more productive for you to do right now? I can find a screwdriver on my own."

It shouldn't have been possible, but Megan looked even more gleeful.

"Grow up," Rory muttered as they turned into the kitchen.

That room was empty, too. The counters were spotless and gleamed under the overhead lights.

"You're the one acting like a sixteen-year-old virgin around him." Megan followed her into the storage room.

Rory slammed shut the drawer she'd just opened. "Remind me why we're friends?"

"Because nobody watches your back like I do," Megan said tartly.

Rory's shoulders slumped. She looked at Megan, contrite. "I know." She pressed her hands on top of the counter and inhaled deeply.

"You are making too big a deal about this." Megan pulled open a drawer and poked through it. "If you've got the itch, scratch it. What's the harm?"

"He's a guest and he could buy us out," she said in a fierce whisper.

"So what? He's a man who has your stirrups all twisted up." Megan lifted an ice pick, giving it a considering look. "When's the last time that happened? The last time you were a mass of *quivering loins*." She drew out the words with dramatic flair.

Rory nearly choked. "There's no quivering going on."

"My foot." Megan tossed aside the ice pick and opened another drawer. "Why are we looking for a screwdriver in here? It's all kitchen stuff. Admit it. You just needed to put some space between you and the delectable developer."

"If you think he's so delectable, *you* do something about it."

"Noah's more my speed." Megan winked. "Young. Lots of energy."

"I need to disinfect my ears now." If she could just remember where she'd seen that screwdriver. "Guest. Remember? Hands off. Besides, Noah's a boy."

"Gage, on the other hand, is all man," Megan countered as if Rory had played right into her hands. "And screw the rules. The world isn't going to stop rotating if you just happen to break your sexual fast with a guest! He's not Jon, for Pete's sake! You don't have to be looking for Mr. Right. Gage strikes me as a great Mr. Right Now."

Rory pressed her palms to her hot cheeks. "It's bad for business."

"Yeah, well, the business hasn't been so good lately!"

One more thing she already knew. "Right now, all I care about is keeping Bitsy and Bobby Pith happy. You know how it works. One good wedding begets another. That's as much as I can concentrate on right now." She snapped her fingers. "I remember now. It was behind the bar." She strode back through the kitchen, flipping off the lights as they went.

The sight of people on the deck outside the soaring windows had her stopping short. "Well, that's just perfect." She gestured. "They're coming back already. Do what you can to stall them for a while yet."

"How am I supposed to do that?"

"From what I've seen of this crowd so far? Just tell them the bar is open." Then she jogged out of the room and back to the office.

Gage had moved to her chair, and he looked up at her when she entered.

It was jarring to see him sitting at the desk, and her footsteps faltered. The only person to sit behind her father's desk in years had been her. "I didn't get the screwdriver. But they're starting to come back, so I'm going to have to settle for what's already done." She retrieved a crate containing custom tote bags from the closet and set it on the couch. After counting the bags, she went back for another dozen.

Gage had left the desk, and his hands brushed

hers as he took the new totes from her when she emerged.

She stopped in surprise as she turned toward the desk to get what she'd prepared so far.

"I finished printing the schedules," he said.

"I see that." She picked up the tidy stack—more than double the size that she'd left. "How did you do it?"

"Made an adjustment to the printer configuration. Overrides everything." He looked at the bags on the couch. "One for each bag?"

"Yes."

As if it were a perfectly ordinary thing for him to do, he began doling out the schedules among the bags. She grabbed the stack of directories, following along behind him.

They could hear voices from the great room now. Laughter. Music when someone turned on the sound system.

She darted back into the closet for the child activity sets and added them on top of the crate. They were color-coded by age range and filled with appropriate games and crafts. She'd learned a long time ago that the easiest way to keep kids happy was to keep them occupied. She pulled on her coat, Gage grabbed the crates and she led the way to the rear of the building where the laundry was located. At the sight of the rolling bins still filled with sheets and towels, her lips tightened.

Before she could hide her reaction, Gage noticed.

His gaze followed hers. "Frannie's supposed to be in charge of all that."

There was no point denying what was perfectly obvious. She pushed through the door leading outside, and it closed heavily behind them.

They stored the stuff in the cargo box of the one UTV parked there and set off. She flipped on the heater even though it wouldn't do a lot to combat the chilly night air, not without one of the cold weather enclosure kits they installed every year. The weather had been so up-and-down lately that she wasn't sure when the time would be right for them.

"What happens when we get to the Uptown Camp?"

"We'll put totes in each room."

"One per?"

"One per adult." She veered around the cabins and sped up. "Each child gets a box. The directory that I printed will tell us who gets what and where it belongs."

Their shoulders collided when she hit a bump and he grabbed the roll bar. But his shoulder stayed pressed against hers.

He was warm. Warmer than the feeble puffs from the heater vents. As distracting as he was, his presence also felt strangely comforting. The same way it had been comforting when he handed her the damp towel to wipe her face that afternoon.

It seemed like days ago by this point.

"How often does this happen?"

Since she'd felt companionable comfort from a man besides her father and Bart? Never.

She shook herself and focused on the present. "Sorry?"

"Parties arriving early. Confirmations for the wrong number of guests."

She fought back her instinctive burst of defensiveness. "You own resorts all over the country. You know how it goes. Some people operate on the spur of the moment. They don't plan ahead. They don't make advance reservations."

"And during high season, those people would be out of luck. If there are no vacancies, there are no vacancies."

"Well, this isn't our high season."

"When is Angel River's high season?"

At least he hadn't asked if they even had one. "End of May to the middle of September. And then again from late December through February if the snow is good. I've been thinking about your idea for a flash promotion. And I, uh, I think we should do it." She glanced at him. "But to answer your question, generally people don't show up on the wrong day, and particularly not for something as important as a destination wedding."

"Or with additional walk-ins in the party."

"Not to this extent." They'd reached the fork in the camp loop. "A few times a year, we'll have someone show up just because they've been out exploring and they've stumbled on us. It's rare when we actually have to turn someone away." He and his brother were perfect examples. "The Pith party isn't a disaster." She wanted to convince herself of that as much as him. "I just don't like being caught unprepared like this. We'll spend their entire visit making up for what they consider to be our error, even though it wasn't. It's not a position I like being in."

"Think they did it deliberately?"

Her foot unconsciously eased on the gas as she gaped at him. "Who would do such a thing?"

"You're comping all of them an extra day and cutting a deal for the extra eighteen guests for more than a week. You think the Piths don't know how much they're saving?"

She hadn't told him about that decision, so she could only assume that Megan had. "You think I should charge them full board?"

"Does it matter what I think?"

She focused on the road for a while. "No," she said finally. Truthfully. "I don't think it does matter." Her voice grew firmer. "I did what needed to be done, and I'm not going to worry about it anymore."

It was too dark to see his expression, but for some reason, she thought she'd pleased him.

At least until he spoke again. "How often does Frannie let you down?"

"She doesn't let me down. Exactly."

"You didn't expect to see those sheets and towels in the laundry."

She flexed her cold fingers around the steering wheel. She should have worn gloves. "We're shorthanded. Everybody is pushed to the limit." She wished she'd taken the time to dump the sheets and towels in the wash before they'd left the lodge. They'd still need to be dealt with when she got back.

"You need help."

She hit the brakes, bringing the utility vehicle to a juddering stop in front of the Homestead lodge. She supposed she should be glad he hadn't started in again on why she was even running the place. "Finding the right people to live and work out here isn't exactly easy. Wymon is *way* smaller than Weaver. That's the closest town to the ranch you bought, right?" Afraid he might bring up his friend the spa owner, she quickly hopped out of the vehicle. "I'm sure you'll have an easier time finding and keeping staff."

"Have you ever been to Weaver?"

"Sure. Wymon High plays football against the schools in Weaver and Braden. That's not too far from Weaver—"

"I know where Braden is. My attorney's from there. I'm pretty sure you didn't play high school football." His voice turned dry. "Cheerleader?"

She laughed shortly as she poked through a bag in search of a directory. "Hardly. Marching band. There were a whopping twenty of us."

"What did you play?"

"Trombone." She gave him a sharp look. "What?"

"Nothing." He lifted his hands peaceably. "Just that you are one surprise after another."

Directory in hand, she pulled out her master key. The main entrance wasn't locked, but all of the interior rooms would be. "Grab a handful of bags." As he gathered as many totes as he could, she did the same, stacking the loops like bracelets that went all the way past her elbow, and they went inside.

Soft lights came on automatically as they walked through the central common area, where the focal point was an enormous stone fireplace. It was surrounded by overstuffed chairs arranged in cozy groupings.

"That," Gage said, "is a lot of luggage."

The pile that Megan had left was far more orderly than she'd implied. But it did take up a considerable amount of floor space, entirely obscuring the long reception counter behind it.

"Fifty-plus people," she reminded him. "Ten days. Not to mention a wedding. Weddings always mean a lot more luggage." She gestured to the wing branching off to the left of the fireplace. "We can start over there."

They quickly settled into a rhythm—Gage unlocking the door and Rory leaving the welcome packages inside. It also gave her one last chance to smooth a wrinkled quilt here. To straighten a stray pillow there.

They finished the first floor and went up the stairs to the second, working their way back to the wing right of the fireplace, then back down to the first floor again. Gage only had to return to the utility vehicle once for more totes.

When they were done in the main building, Rory turned on the big gas logs in the fireplace, made sure the protective glass was in place and they moved on to the individual cabins, situated in a wide circle around the swimming pool. He took over driving, which let her nip in and out as she delivered the rest of the totes and craft boxes.

She'd just finished the very last one when she saw the distinctive pinpoint of headlights off in the distance. There was a whole string of them.

Gage noticed, too. "They're on the way."

Adrenaline surging, she hopped in beside him. "Drive over to that shed." She gestured at the shadowy structure. "On the other side of the horseshoe pits."

He didn't question why. He just hit the gas and drove around to the shed. She got out again and nearly dropped her passkey in her hurry to get the door open. Inside, she flipped a switch, and the hanging bulbs spanning the expanse of the pool area came on, bathing the water and everything else in a gentle dance of golden light. She hit another switch, and the automatic cover on the big hot tub rumbled softly as it rolled open. Steam billowed as warm water met cold air. A third master switch started the water churning softly. If the controls next to the tub weren't used, the master would automatically shut off in a few hours.

She relocked the shed and jogged back to him. "Let's get out of here," she said breathlessly. "If you drive up behind the cabins, there's a hiking path that's wide enough to drive on. It's the long way around, but at least nobody'll see us."

Soon he was guiding the vehicle up the narrow ridge well beyond the cabins, stopping and turning off the headlights when she told him.

The panorama of Angel River Ranch was spread out below. The soft glow of the main lodge off in the distance contrasted with the brighter one from the nearby Uptown Camp. "We're up behind Angel Camp." He sounded surprised as he pointed. "That's your cabin, isn't it?"

"Yes." They watched the string of headlights from the wedding party work their way nearer. Above them, stars glittered in the inky sky.

"My mom's favorite spot might have been the lookout," she admitted softly, "but this spot is mine. My studio is only a few yards away from here."

She felt his look. But he didn't comment. "Why didn't you want any of them to see us?" he asked instead.

She pushed her cold hands into her coat pockets, hunching toward the heater vents again. "My mother made all these little touches seem effortless," she finally answered. "*She* was never once caught unprepared. Not where guests were concerned."

"Is that why you were so determined to get this all done tonight? Trying to live up to the bar she set?"

She looked at him. As bright as the sky was with stars, his eyes were still dark, unreadable in the shadows. "You said it yourself. Why am I managing Angel River? I'm an artist." She looked away. "Or I was. For a while." She shrugged, pushing her hair out of her eyes as she watched the procession of UTV headlights. "No matter how bad I am at this, Angel River is a special place. It doesn't matter what kind of problems we had today—I still want everyone to leave here feeling that, too. I guess I just don't want someone seeing behind the curtain," she admitted.

"You want them to only see the magic," he said quietly.

"Yes." She looked at him again. "That's it exactly."

"You're safe, then." His voice was low. Deep.

Even as impossible as it was to see his expression, her heart still lurched. She could make out the shape of his lips and couldn't make herself look away. "Why?"

He lifted his hand, and she couldn't help starting when he brushed her hair away from her cheek. "Because magic is all I see."

Then he leaned closer and lightly brushed those perfect, perfect lips once, twice, across hers.

"And for the record—" his voice dropped another notch "—you're not bad at anything."

And he kissed her a third time.

Chapter Ten

"Stupid," Gage muttered for the tenth time as he walked to his cabin from the main lodge. "Stupid, stupid, freaking stupid."

What had possessed him to kiss her?

One minute she was sitting there, looking vulnerable and talking about her mom, and the next he was kissing her.

"Stupid," he said again through his teeth as he stomped up the cabin's wooden steps.

"Pathetic, too." Noah's voice cut through the dark, and Gage realized his brother was sitting in one of the wooden rockers on the porch. "I've heard of old dudes like you talking to themselves, but now I see it's true."

Noah hadn't turned on any lights, but the stars

were just as bright here as they were up on that ridge beyond the Uptown Camp. Gage could see the slender bottle in his brother's hand just fine.

Same as he'd been able to see the shock in Rory's eyes when she'd jerked back after he'd kissed her.

Stupid. He managed not to voice it, but the word still circled around inside his head.

So maybe his voice came out colder than it should have. "Better not be anything stronger than root beer in that bottle."

"And if it is?"

Gage's fists curled. He didn't want to fight with Noah. But it was easier to justify falling into that familiar routine than his behavior with Rory. "Then we can call it quits right now and you can spend the holidays in a jail cell."

Noah didn't reply. He just lifted the bottle and took a long, long pull on it.

Gage wanted to yank it out of Noah's hands. Instead, he wrapped his hands around the top rail surrounding the porch. "Rory said to tell you thanks for helping out today."

Noah lowered the bottle. It was pretty much predictable at this point that Noah reacted more positively to the slightest mention of Rory than he did to anything else.

"That where you've been?" Noah's voice went tight. "With her?"

"I helped her get some things done for the group that came in."

And you kissed her.

He thumped his palm on the wooden rail, trying to beat back the voice inside his head. "She needs more help than just mixing drinks."

"What's your point?"

His jaw ached from the way he'd been clenching it so much lately. "What else do you know how to do? Anything besides the cocktails and the horses?"

Noah didn't answer. He lifted his bottle again.

Gage looked across to the lodge. There were lights on in several of the rooms. One of them would be the laundry, where Rory had headed when they'd gotten back to the lodge.

After he'd shocked her into silence by his damn stupidity.

She hadn't said a single word. Not after he'd kissed her. Not on the drive back down to the lodge. And not when she'd used her key to get into the laundry room and disappeared inside like the devil was on her heels.

He'd put her in a hell of a position with that kiss. Worse than anything the Piths had done, that was for damn sure. Particularly after he'd witnessed how hard she'd worked to salvage that situation. All to keep the clients happy.

Add thoughtless to stupid.

She was never going to relax around him again. The last thing he wanted was for her to think he believed he had some sort of right to touch her, just because he'd paid a fortune for her time and for the lodging.

Stupid. Stupid, freaking stupid.

He should have cleared it up immediately. Promised her it would never happen again.

He realized Noah was silently watching him. Probably wondering what the hell had gotten into him.

Fine. Whatever. Noah was Noah. He always would be.

Gage shoved open the cabin door.

"It's cider," Noah said abruptly.

Gage froze.

"*Plain* apple cider," Noah added darkly. "Chef Bart makes it."

"I know," Gage said slowly. "Rory's father drinks a glass in the mornings along with his oatmeal." He let the door close and shoved his hands into his pockets. He could feel the worn edges of the cigarette pack with his thumb. "Was it hard? Working behind the bar earlier?"

When Noah didn't answer, he squelched another sigh, feeling older than he should. "I'm glad it's cider," he said.

But he didn't go so far as to admit he was proud of Noah. Then his brother would know for certain that Gage had lost his marbles.

He pushed open the door again.

"It wasn't a piece of cake." Noah's voice was low.

Barely audible. "And I don't know how to do anything else."

Gage stopped, one foot across the threshold. Noah's words could have sounded self-pitying. But instead, his brother's tone was matter-of-fact. "That's hard to believe."

"Why?" The question was more like Noah. Full of insolence. "Because *you* know how to do everything?"

Gage didn't know how to rewind the last hour. How to undo that kiss.

He wearily rubbed the back of his neck and controlled the impulse to pull out the cigarettes. "I don't know how to help you," he admitted.

"I don't want your help."

He sighed deeply. "It's not a choice, Noah."

He could see the grimace on his brother's face. "Because you promised my mother you'd take care of me."

"She was my mother, too."

"And it would kill her to see what's become of me," Noah muttered. "That's what you're thinking."

"Althea Stanton was made of sturdier stuff than that," Gage countered. She'd survived his father's premature death. Then Noah's father's death. "It wouldn't have killed her." It had taken a massive stroke that hit out of the blue several years ago to do that. "She'd have just been mighty pissed off with you. And she would've kicked your hind end until you could recognize for yourself what the right path looked like."

"There's nothing I know how to do that is gonna help Rory."

"A pair of willing hands is what she needs the most. That and a person who doesn't sleep past noon."

When Noah didn't respond, Gage turned to go inside. "You're my brother," he said abruptly. "*That's* why it's not a choice."

Leaving Noah to chew on that, he went inside and closed the door.

The fireplace was cold and black, and he thought of the fire that Rory had left burning for the wedding group. About the way she'd bent over backward to accommodate them. He had employees to handle all those sorts of things at his resorts.

He turned the control on the fireplace, and a flame immediately began licking at the realistic-looking logs. He'd always preferred a real wood fire to a gas-fueled one. But he had to admit that it was still a welcoming touch.

He left the fire burning for his brother and went upstairs. But once in his room, he didn't go to bed. He stood at the dark window and stared out at the infinite stars.

Rory could smell the coffee when she entered the lodge kitchen the next morning.

"Sorry I'm late," she greeted Bart, who was

standing behind one of the stainless steel prep tables, folding a perfect rectangle of pale dough into thirds. "I overslept." She crossed to the coffeepot on the stove, filled a clean mug and took an appreciative sip. "Oh, yesssss. I still don't know what your secret is."

"Actually brewing it," he said dryly.

She tied an apron around her waist and washed her hands before joining him at the table. He'd been busy while she'd been snoozing her alarm clock into oblivion. Not only did he have his chocolate croissants well underway, but several batches of dough were already waiting in bowls. "What do you need me to do?"

"Knead," he joked. "Same thing as always." He nudged one of the bowls toward her.

Using a clean cup, she scooped flour out of the enormous canister and moved farther down the long table. She sprinkled the surface with flour, dumped the sticky dough out of the bowl and lightly sprinkled more flour on top of it.

It would be a lot easier to just add baked goods to the supply order, but there simply was nothing better than what Bart made by hand.

He didn't even use a bread machine. By hand literally meant by hand, and she'd been rolling and kneading bread dough in this kitchen with him since her mother was alive. She was no great shakes as a cook, but after years of practice under his watchful eye, at least she could do this part.

But Rory did feel bad for being nearly an hour late. She didn't have to ask how much extra they were making because of the Pith group. She could see for herself there were three times more rattan cane proofing baskets stacked to one side than usual.

Bart didn't just make beautiful loaves of sourdough bread, though that was his primary staple. He made marbled rye bread. Seven grain. Italian olive. He made dinner rolls. Sandwich rolls. Pretzels. Bagels. The occasional quick bread, though he usually made those later in the week. But always, always the most delicious chocolate-filled croissants on the planet.

Spending these early hours with the chef—pressing, folding, turning the dough—while the kitchen smelled of yeast and coffee was as close to healing meditation as Rory had ever gotten outside of sitting at her potter's wheel.

But that morning, all she could think about was the night before. About Gage.

She couldn't believe the way she'd acted. As if she'd never been kissed. It hadn't even been that much of a kiss.

Actually, it was three kisses.

Her lips tingled in remembrance.

The kiss—okay, the three kisses—had nearly been chaste.

She'd overreacted. So much so that she wasn't sure how she'd ever recover from the embarrassment.

It wasn't as if she could avoid Gage until he left

Angel River. The man was going to be there for weeks yet.

"So why'd you oversleep?" Bart's voice cut into her self-flagellation.

She realized her dough that had started out wet and sticky had already turned smooth and elastic under her palms. Overkneading was a bad, bad sin. She walked over to the stack of baskets. "A person oversleeps now and then."

"Not you."

"Maybe it's the rain." It had started falling again when she'd finally left the lodge after she'd finished laundering the sheets the night before. The rain hadn't stopped since. Even now, she could hear its soft drum against the kitchen windows. But at least it wasn't like the downpour they'd had the previous week.

She snatched a basket from the stack and carried it back to her working area. She sprinkled the basket with more flour, rubbing it into the crevices between the circular rattan coils so the dough, once raised, wouldn't stick when it was turned out. "It was a busy night last night. You know. With the wedding party arriving the way they did." She winced, knowing how defensive she sounded.

"Everything's going to be just fine with that group," Bart said calmly. "We've juggled twice as many people many, many times. Remember—oh, it has to be nearly five years now, because the lookout deck was brand-new—when we had three weddings going on during the same weekend?"

She gently placed the round of dough inside the basket, smiling despite herself. She'd been so horrified when her dad had accepted the concurrent wedding reservations.

They'd had a full contingent of staff, full-time and seasonal. And even *she* had been pressed into service. "I remember. Killy was just a baby, and I was trying to nurse him between racing around between the three events." She smiled. "Remember the Torres reception at the Overlook Camp?"

"It was so hot, the icing on the wedding cake melted and the tiers started sliding and—"

"The best man fell into the river trying to catch it," she finished. "Hard to believe we can laugh about that now."

"Let enough time go by, and a person can laugh about all sorts of things." Bart shook his head, chuckling. "Try as I might, I could not convince that sweet little bride that whipped icing was a bad idea on a hot June day." He pointed the end of his rolling pin at her. "Mark my words." The pin punctuated each word. "Won't be long and you'll be laughing about *this* wedding, too." Then his gaze went past Rory. "Wasn't sure you were going to make it."

That was how much notice Rory had.

She felt a fine shiver on the back of her neck and turned to see Gage entering the kitchen. His unshaven jaw was darker than it had been the day before. He was wearing a black mock-neck sweater with a short red zipper that was open halfway down his neck and faded blue jeans.

Just looking at him made something inside her feel weak.

"Wasn't sure I was, either," Gage answered. His dark gaze slid over her before he pulled a mug from the shelf and turned to the stove to fill it with coffee. "I've had more nights that lasted until four in the morning than days that started at four."

With some difficulty, Rory looked away from the black knit sweater hugging his wide shoulders. She felt too warm, and when she scraped her work area clean, her hand shook.

Coffee mug in hand, Gage turned and went over to the table midway between her and Chef Bart. "Quite the production. Smells like a bakery."

"Wait until we start pulling the goods out of the ovens," Bart said. "Takes me back to my *boulangerie* days in Paris." He kissed the tips of his fingers. "Superb."

"Can't wait," Gage murmured. His eyes were as dark as the block of Belgian chocolate that Bart was unwrapping. "When were you in France?"

"My early twenties," Bart said, looking reminiscent. "I studied at Le Cordon Bleu." He gave a broad wink. "And the lovely French girls."

"I've studied a few French girls myself," Gage said, smiling slightly.

Maybe *Sybil* had been in France as well as Switzerland.

Rory flipped the dough in front of her and mashed it beneath the heel of her palm.

"How'd you get from Paris to Angel River?"

"A woman, of course," Bart answered him.

"That'll happen," Gage said. "Or so I've heard."

Rory flipped the dough again, accidentally knocking over her cup of flour. A cloud of white puffed up around her. "Can I talk to you for a minute?"

Gage looked at her over the rim of his mug, and she jerked her head in the direction of the storage room. She didn't wait for him to answer; she just walked through the doorway.

She pushed the door closed when he joined her, even though she knew she'd have to deal with Bart's unrelenting curiosity as a result.

Her stomach was in knots, and her entire body felt flushed. She would rather have been anywhere other than there. Maybe. Because closed in the storage room with him, she noticed just how good he smelled. "Look," she said raggedly, "about last night."

His lips thinned. "Yeah. About that."

"I shouldn't have—"

"I shouldn't have—"

Her gaze collided with his as they both broke off. Feeling even more awkward, she rocked on her tennis shoes and tucked her dusty fingertips in the back pockets of her jeans.

He gestured with his mug. "You go."

Go? She'd like to go out the back door and keep right on going. But that wouldn't solve anything. She drew in a breath. Held it for a moment. Then went for broke. "I shouldn't have reacted the way I did," she said as she exhaled. "I just, uh, well, you just, uh—"

"Surprised you."

He had. With the way he'd read her mind. About the Angel River magic. And about the kiss. She'd wanted him to kiss her. As illogical as it was, she'd still wanted it. "Yes. I…panicked. I'm sorry."

If anything, his expression turned even grimmer. "I noticed. You don't have to worry, though. It won't happen again. You have my word on that."

She tried to smile. Considering she felt worse than ever, she had doubts she succeeded.

Of course it would never happen again. Why would a man like him want a repeat of that abysmal moment? Especially after all her claims about not getting involved with guests. She gave a jerky nod. "Then we'll just…just erase the board as if it never happened."

As if *that* were remotely possible.

She sidled around him to reach for the door to the kitchen. "You don't really need to see how Bart makes his bread. I know I put it on the list when you first got here, but it doesn't have anything to do with running a guest ranch."

"Maybe not. But Bart mentioned it at dinner last

night, and you said extra hands were welcome. And I couldn't sleep. So." He held out one of his hands, wide palm up, long fingers spread. "Extra."

She hadn't been able to sleep, either. Not until it was too late and she was supposed to get up.

We could have been not sleeping together.

She quickly looked away, hoping he wasn't reading her mind, and yanked open the door. "If you're really offering extra hands, how are you at folding towels?"

"The ones from the laundry last night?"

"I finished the sheets last night, but I didn't get the towels into the wash until this morning. They should be ready for the dryer by now."

"I'll take care of it." He set his mug on the counter and strode out of the kitchen. Almost as if he couldn't wait to get away.

She chewed the inside of her cheek. Relieved. Of course she was relieved.

"You want to tell ol' Bart what's going on?"

She jerked guiltily and looked at the chef. He was babysitting his chocolate at the stove. "Sorry?"

"Haven't seen you so distracted by a man since you went to the prom with Donny Thomas."

"Donny Thomas!" She hadn't thought about her high school crush in forever. "I'd have thought you'd have said Jon. I *did* marry him, at least."

"And I'd say he was a total waste of space on this planet, except that he did give you Killy." Bart turned off the flame under his pan and stirred the glossy chocolate, watching it ribbon off his wooden spoon. Then he tapped the spoon gently and held it out to her.

She took it, just as he'd known she would. She sucked some of the chocolate from the tip, then stirred it around inside her coffee mug, watching the rest slowly disappear in a swirl. "He's a guest."

"He's a man who's got your flutters in a twitter."

She smiled reluctantly. "Flutters in a twitter?"

"Jugglies in a quiver? Wannas in a whirl?"

She rolled her eyes, laughing slightly. "Worry about your own love life, Bart."

"So you admit you're thinking *love life*." He gave a satisfied nod and wiped his hands on the towel wrapped around his waist before reaching for his rolling pin again.

"I'm not thinking about anything besides getting through all of this bread dough," she said and plopped the uneven lump she'd abandoned into another proofing basket. Then she scraped her work area clean and started on yet another batch.

Before long, Gage returned. But she had herself under control by then. Or else she was sedated by a suitable amount of chocolate-spiked coffee by then.

She didn't even shiver, flutter or whirl when he cleared a space on the table, washed his hands, then scooped some of her spilled flour to dust his own work area.

Okay, so maybe she did stare a little.

What else could she do when he pushed up the

sleeves of his sweater, tipped out a bowl and began working a batch of sweet roll dough as if he'd done it for years?

Only catching the delighted expression on Bart's face as he watched her got her moving again on her own task.

Soon enough, all of the baskets were full and resting beneath the sackcloth towels spread over them. Once the loaves had risen, Bart would turn them out to bake, but the pretty imprint of the basket coils would remain.

While Rory had portioned dough for rolls and twisted ropes into giant pretzels, Bart had shown Gage how to form the bagels. Those were now resting on sheets stacked in the upper half of a tall rolling rack. The bottom half of the rack contained Rory's efforts. Chef Bart would take care of baking everything throughout the rest of the day.

She was cleaning up the worktable and Gage was sweeping the floor when she heard Killy's voice. A moment later, he and her dad entered. The real surprise, though, was the sight of Gage's brother ambling along after them. His long hair was hanging down around the shoulders of his dull gray hoodie, and he looked as though he'd just woken up.

"Is there coffee?" he asked.

"Sure." Rather than make a big deal about his unexpected presence, Rory handed him a clean mug, indicating the pot on the stove, and then crouched down to grab Killy and give him a quick nuzzle. His hair was sparkling with raindrops. "Good morning, handsome. Did you have a good night with Grandpa?"

"We watched a Christmas show this morning. It was a cartoon about Frosty the Snowman." Killy squirmed out of her hold and ran over to peer at the first batch of croissants that were already cooled and drizzled with chocolate. "Can I write a letter to Santa now?"

From the corner of her eye, she could see the wary looks passing between Gage and his brother. "We need to get through Thanksgiving before we start worrying about letters to Santa."

"Thanksgiving's just turkey. Santa brings presents." He sneaked a finger up to touch one of the croissants but snatched his hand back, looking innocent when Bart reached over his head to move the cooling tray to a safer location. "Can I have pancakes for breakfast?"

"You can have pancakes only if you eat eggs first. Because you need some protein, too." She held out her hand toward him. "Let's go home so I can fix it for you."

The way her son's expression dropped was almost comical. "But Chef Bart—"

"Has a lot to do this morning for the actual *guests*. He's too busy to make you pancakes." They'd already spent hours in the kitchen just preparing baked goods. He still needed to start on his preparations for the actual meals he'd be serving that day.

"But your pancakes are…"

She raised her eyebrows, and Killy's voice trailed off. He wrinkled his nose but took her hand without further protest.

"Frannie called me this morning," her dad said before she could take a step toward the storeroom and the back exit.

"Hope it was to apologize for not getting the sheets and towels done yesterday."

"She said they've all got chicken pox. The kids and her."

"Chicken pox!" Rory cried in dismay. The timing couldn't have been worse. "She's sure?"

"You know it's been going around. Damon probably brought it home from school."

If Damon had, so had Killy. She looked toward Gage and Noah. "Please tell me you've had them already."

Noah shrugged. He was showing as much interest in the croissants as her son had. "I can't remember."

"You were four," Gage said abruptly. He glanced at Rory, seemingly oblivious to the frown that crossed his brother's face. "We've both had 'em."

"Thank goodness *you've* already had them, too." She brushed Killy's hair out of his eyes. So had she when she was a kid.

"You painted me with the pink stuff that stopped me being all scratchy." Killy squirmed out from under her hand. "Damon and me were gonna build a fort today, though."

"Damon and I, and I'm afraid that's not going to happen today, sweetie."

"Not *you* and Damon. *Me* and Damon."

She shot a glance toward Gage at the faint sound he made. But he was focused hard on his coffee. Noah, on the other hand, watched like they were a tennis match, his head bobbing back and forth.

"I was counting on Astrid to help mind the Uptown kids. Bitsy Pith's expecting it." She looked to her father. "Do you think Toonie—"

Rory's father shook his head. "You know how shy she is. She can barely look Bart in the face when she drops off the fresh milk, and she grew up here. Plus she's too young."

"She's fourteen," Rory argued, but in her heart she knew her dad was right.

The day's offering of activities had changed slightly because of the rain. Sunday was always a day off for the horses. But the other outdoor activities—climbing Angel's Lookout, ATV rides and disk golf—were out.

Instead, the default was a friendly poker tournament in the lodge or square dancing and a leatherworking class in the activity barn. If the rain continued for longer, they had more alternatives waiting in the wings.

It was going to be interesting, to say the least, where Bitsy Pith was concerned. But the woman could hardly blame them for the weather.

Rory looked to her father. "Are you up to monitoring the poker games?"

"Of course." He looked vaguely insulted that she'd asked.

She really was batting a thousand.

"Killy will have to come with me while I take care of the housekeeping. Marni's going to have to handle the square dancing. Megan's on the leather craft." She glanced at Bart. "That leaves you without any kitchen help for most of the day."

"No, it doesn't." Gage had lifted his nose from the mug. He raised his palm again, his eyes capturing hers. "Extra."

"He does know how to make a breakfast burrito," Bart said. Of everyone there, he seemed the least concerned about the situation.

Gage was still watching her. "Unless you need me more."

Flitters. Twitters. Juggles galore.

She tore her eyes away, focusing instead on the rain-streaked windows behind him. She knew he meant with the housekeeping but that didn't stop her nerve endings from acting out their own personal Fourth of July fireworks.

Only the knowledge that everyone was watching her helped her keep her wits together. "I can get Uptown cleaned this afternoon while everyone's out for activities."

"That doesn't solve the problem of who's watching the kiddos," her father prompted.

"Right." She went over to the coffeepot, but Noah had emptied it. "Seven kids. All too young to be left to their own devices while their parents go out and play."

Noah suddenly spoke. "Let 'em build forts." He looked vaguely uncomfortable with the attention he'd earned, and he focused on Killy. "That's what you were going to do, wasn't it?"

Killy turned his pleading eyes to Rory. "Can we? I could do it, too, right?"

"Homestead's common room has plenty of space," her dad said. "They can either use the furniture to build the forts or push it all aside and set up the pup tents we've got in storage."

"*Real* tents!" Killy practically bounced on his toes at the prospect.

Rory wasn't sure she liked that suggestion. "But who do I put in charge? Killy? Without Frannie and Astrid, I don't have enough people to—"

"I'll do it," Noah said, and once again, all eyes turned to him. "How hard can it be?"

Beneath that bit of bravado, Rory was certain she saw uncertainty. Uncertainty and the same desire to please that she saw so often in her little boy's eyes. Noah just worked harder to disguise it. "There will be *seven* kids," she felt compelled to caution.

"Eight," Killy piped excitedly.

No matter how much compassion she felt for Noah, she wasn't thrilled at the prospect of her son thinking he'd found his own new personal superhero. Which was exactly how Killy was looking at Noah.

"Eight," she repeated. She reminded herself that Noah had pitched in the day before when the wedding party arrived. Helped to keep them entertained and happy with cocktails in their hands.

But cocktails weren't children. She couldn't chance any mistakes where they were concerned.

She looked toward Gage.

Nothing in his expression helped her feel any more confident, because he was staring at his brother as if he didn't recognize him.

She turned back to Noah again. "Are you sure?"

He might look as though he'd just rolled out of bed, but his eyes were clear. His gaze steady. Remarkably similar to his brother's despite the different coloring. "It matters, doesn't it?"

She felt a little sigh escape. People tended to live up—or down—to expectations. Maybe he just needed someone to have some faith in him.

She could save cleaning Homestead until he was there building forts—or pitching tents—and babysitting. At least she'd be on the premises.

She nodded. "Yes," she said. "It matters."

Chapter Eleven

The rain continued.

And with each passing day, Rory felt the mounting blame that Bitsy and Bobby Pith sent her way. Because it seemed they really *could* blame her for the weather.

Fortunately, the bride- and groom-to-be were much more adaptable. As were the rest of their wedding party and the guests. Once Rory had a chance to actually get to know her, Sabrina Larissa Pith turned out to be the least Bridezilla-ish bride who had ever visited Angel River.

It was the only reason that Rory managed not to lose her mind when Bitsy Pith—the *mom*zilla of all time—rained a fresh batch of demands on their heads.

For the fourth day running.

Bitsy started with a request for all of the mealtimes to be changed, because her "delicate" system just was not accustomed to the different time zone.

Evidently, she couldn't digest her mimosas two hours earlier than she was used to back home in Florida.

Rory sat behind her desk, her hands clasped atop her heavily doodled blotter as her mind took a quick little vacation, imagining Bitsy Pith far, far away.

"…and you have to do something about this ridiculous weather," Bitsy was saying when Rory tuned back in for a quick check. The woman wasn't running out of steam at all. "Ludo is arriving tomorrow. How is he supposed to make Sabby look beautiful enough for the cover of *Miam-I-Do* magazine when it's all gray outside? I *knew* this was a bad idea having the wedding here, but my daughter just *had* to insist." She was pacing in front of the desk. "I had everything all arranged for the club *next* year, but no." She slashed her hand through the air. "That wasn't good enough. She had to get married *this* year."

For a moment, Rory watched her pace back and forth, back and forth. Bitsy was wearing a sleeveless pink blouse and white slacks, which might work in Florida at this time of year but was an insane choice for northern Wyoming in the middle of November. There were spatters of mud around the hems of her cropped white slacks, and Rory could easily see the goose bumps on Bitsy's thin arms.

"Would you like something warm to drink?" Only after she'd asked the question did she realize that she'd spoken right over whatever it was that Bitsy was blithering on about. "Coffee? Hot chocolate?" Not that the woman seemed to need any more stimulants. It was also too early in the day for something stronger—though that never seemed to stop her husband.

Or a lot of their guests, actually. They were definitely a group who knew how to have a good time. The rainy days hadn't stopped them in the least.

Bitsy planted her palms on the desk, the sharp points of her vermilion fingernails pressed like daggers against the wood. She leaned over Rory. *"What I want is this effing weather cleared up,"* she screeched.

Startled, Rory rolled her chair back and bumped the credenza behind her. Definitely no more stimulants for Bitsy Pith. "Maybe some herbal tea would be a good—"

"If I'm offered another cup of herbal tea—" Bitsy bared her teeth "—I'm going to scream."

Rory decided it was prudent not to point out that she'd already done so. "Mrs. Pith, I understand your frustration, but—"

"You understand nothing!" Bitsy leaned over the desk even farther. "Do you *care* at all that you are *ruining* my daughter's wedding?"

"Mother!"

Bitsy jumped as though she'd been bitten on her bare, mud-spattered ankles.

Sabrina entered the office, casting Rory an apologetic look. She was as different from her mother as night and day. Bitsy was a tall, bleached rail of nerve. Sabrina was shorter than Rory, comfortably plump and curvy with a smile that could light a room. She was, without question, head over heels in love with her fiancé and he with her.

She also had more sense than her mother when it came to suitable attire, because Sabrina's jeans were tucked into duck boots, and she wore a bright yellow rain slicker over her flannel shirt.

"Don't look at me like that, Sabby," Bitsy said tearfully. She clutched her daughter to her. "This is *the* most important time of your life! It should be absolutely perfect." She looked reproachfully at Rory over Sabrina's head.

"It *is* perfect." Sabrina gave a light laugh, no doubt meant to reassure her mother. "Dante and I don't care about a little rain."

"But everyone is *dying* of boredom." Bitsy's voice rose again.

With visible effort, Sabrina wriggled out of her mother's tight grasp. She looked a little breathless as she tightened her ponytail and sent Rory another look—this one more embarrassed than the last. "No one is bored, Mother," she soothed with what was obvious long practice. "When is the last time you ate?"

Bitsy threw herself dramatically onto the couch. "Who can eat at the outrageous times these *people*—" she said it as if they were pock-ridden aliens from another planet "—see fit to serve meals?" She dropped a goose-pimpled, bony arm over her eyes.

Rory caught a faint eye roll from Sabrina. "Well, it's brunch time at home. So perhaps a little food. Hmm? For me?"

Bitsy shuddered visibly. "I *suppose* I could try to choke down a little something. For you, darling. You're suffering so much this week as it is."

Rory stood. "I'll send a tray right in for you, Mrs. Pith."

"We can go—"

"No, no, Sabrina. Happy to take care of it." Rory was already halfway to the door and escape. She waved a hand at the couch. "You two just relax." She darted out of the office, only to bump squarely into Noah.

She pressed her finger to her lips. "Shh," she mouthed and grabbed his arm to drag him out of sight of the doorway. She kept hold of him until they reached the great room, where a giant fire was crackling in the fireplace. She'd always been glad the gas logs had only been installed in the Homestead lodge and some of the newer cabins, because she loved a wood fire.

The few guests there seemed to like it, too. The MacArthurs were cozied up together in an over-stuffed love seat near the fireplace, working on a puzzle they'd brought with them. The young couple had replaced Tig and Willow, who had departed two days ago.

On the other side of the fireplace, the Jorgensons were playing backgammon with one of the married couples from the Pith group. They barely gave Rory a glance as she let go of Noah, still aiming for the kitchen.

"Sorry," she finally told him. "Pith emergency." She glanced at him. "What's up?"

"Been thinking about what to do with the kids tomorrow," Noah told her as they turned into the breakfast room.

"Okay." She had been nervous about his ability to handle the kid duty, but he'd come through like a champ. And in the days since—while their parents were busy participating in the daily activities—he'd hosted DVD cartoon fests with the kids in the Homestead lodge and straw-bale mazes and pony rides in the barn. He'd even hauled one of the rowboats up from the river to the barn to play pirates. As far as all the children were concerned—including her own son—Noah was the absolute greatest.

Her eyes skated over the basket of muffins on the wood buffet. Only gluten-free would work for Bitsy, even though Sabrina had told Rory in an aside that her mother wasn't allergic or even remotely gluten sensitive.

Fortunately, Bart was used to accommodating

dietary requests—real or imagined—and had taken to preparing a special "Bitsy basket" just for her.

"I'm thinking art projects," Noah went on.

"Art sounds good. We keep a stock of basic supplies. Paper. Paints. That sort of thing. Just let me know what you need."

She didn't see Bitsy's basket, so she continued into the kitchen. When she caught sight of Gage filling the dishwasher, she prided herself on not breaking stride.

Okay, every nerve ending she possessed tingled, but she didn't trip over her own feet, which had to be a tick in the win column.

"I was thinking we need you," Noah said just as Gage glanced their way.

He gave her a fleeting smile as he leaned over to slide the rack into the washer, his black hair falling into his deep brown eyes.

His hair grew so fast, she thought to herself, mesmerized.

He straightened then, and almost as if he'd been reading her mind, shoved his fingers through his hair, pushing it back off his face. She realized the thin leather wrist wrap they'd made during one of Megan's activities this week had replaced his expensive watch.

It also dawned on her then that she couldn't remember the last time she'd seen him with his phone in hand.

She belatedly focused on Noah. "Sorry, what?"

"What I need is you."

Another rack clattered into the dishwasher.

It took all of her willpower not to look over at Gage again. "Need me for what?"

"You said you went to art school. I don't know anything about that stuff."

She started shaking her head before he'd even finished. "You don't need me, Noah. All you have to do is stick a big sheet of paper and a pot of finger paints in front of kids—doesn't matter *how* old they are— and they'll do the rest. Well, probably better cover every surface that can be covered with plastic first. The paints we have are nontoxic and washable, but finger painting makes a huge mess." She gave him an encouraging pat on the shoulder, stepping around him with the intention of escaping the kitchen. "It's great how you're planning ahead. You've really been a huge help this week."

She made it back through the breakfast room to where the basket of muffins sat on the buffet in all their gluteny glory.

Mocking her.

She spun on her heel and went back into the kitchen.

Avoiding looking at both men, she slapped a serving tray down on the prep table without a word, then yanked open the wide fridge. She pulled out a plastic bin of sliced fresh fruit and filled a small bowl with it. When she added a crystal cup full of yogurt that Bart made from the milk produced by the cows

Seth kept for just that purpose, she caught the look passing between Noah and Gage.

Her cheeks warmed, and she ignored the two of them even harder. She went into the storeroom—it was chillier in there because of the poor weather—and grabbed one of the little stoneware honey pots imprinted with the Angel River logo. When she went back into the kitchen, Bart was entering from the other side. He was wearing a rain slicker and carrying a flat basket full of leafy greens he'd obviously just picked.

"I wasn't thinking of paint so much as clay, Rory." Noah picked up the discussion as if she hadn't ended it. "You did that stuff. Right?"

"You bet she did." Bart set his load next to the tray she was preparing. "I remember the days when we could barely peel her out of her studio."

"That was a long time ago."

"Not that long." He slid the honey pot out of her fingers and held it up. "These were your design."

She snatched it back and set it on the tray with a soft thunk. Since she'd carved the wing in front of her cabin, she'd been thinking more and more about her studio. "A long time ago," she reiterated more for her own benefit than anyone else's.

And then, because she couldn't put it off any longer, she reached around Gage to grab the Bitsy basket.

She saw the amusement in his eyes and was certain that he knew she'd forgotten what she'd come into the kitchen for the first time.

She shot a warning finger in the air between them. "Not one word."

He was hardly containing his smile at this point. "I was just going to ask you how Nelson was faring."

"Nelson!" Amusement overrode everything else. "He wasn't belly up when I got up this morning, so I guess he's managing. Why do you keep asking?"

"Doing my part to keep tabs on the goldfish of the world."

She let out a laugh and escaped with the tray.

What with the rain and the chicken pox, Rory had been depending on Gage lending a willing hand just as much as she had everyone else. Despite having his own business to run from a distance, no less, he'd continued mucking stalls and added hauling firewood daily to all the cabins that burned the real thing. He'd brainstormed ideas with her in the office for the holiday flash deal and then helped her find the best places to advertise it. He helped Bart prep mountains of food in the kitchen and had even run interference a time or two between Rory and the Piths.

Familiarity ought to have helped her gain more control over her reactions where he was concerned, but the reality was just the opposite.

She wasn't thinking of him as a guest. She wasn't thinking of him as the competitor. Or the person with the wherewithal to acquire the ranch if he saw fit to convince her father to sell.

She was just thinking of him. Period.

Day and night. The dreams were even more vivid now. The yank-awake kind that left her breathing hard and her body weak.

She wasn't sure if her subconscious was more or less annoying than Bitsy Pith's constant criticism.

The momzilla was still dramatically draped over the couch when Rory reached the office. She set the tray on the coffee table and smiled at Sabrina. "Feel free to stay here until your mother feels better. But I'm afraid I'm going to have to leave you for the moment."

It was going to be more than a moment, though. The morning activities would be starting soon, and that meant it was time for Rory to gather up the cleaning supplies.

And wasn't it quite a statement to know that she preferred cleaning toilets to spending one more minute in the company of Bitsy Pith?

Sabrina followed her into the corridor. "Rory," she said under her breath, "I want to apologize for my mother again."

Rory shook her head. "Not necessary, Sabrina."

"But it is." She kept pace with Rory. "Dante and I just want to be married. All this wedding stuff—" She waved her hand. "None of it really matters to us."

Rory couldn't help thinking of all the fancy papers. The ribbons. The programs that still had to be dealt with.

"We wanted to elope," Sabrina went on. "But my parents were completely opposed." She spread her hands, looking helpless. "Mother wanted us to wait until next May. Get married at their club with three hundred of their nearest and dearest in attendance. I swear, the day after we told her we were engaged, she already had chosen a date for us and booked it! And it would have been a nightmare."

Rory's steps slowed as they reached the great room. She couldn't help herself. "How did you end up here at Angel River?"

"Dante had a friend who got married here a few years ago. To this day, Matteo and Margo talk about how perfect their wedding was."

She jerked slightly. Surprised. "The Torreses?"

"You remember them?"

Rory couldn't help laughing slightly. Happy weddings—even ones where the best man landed in the river—begot happy weddings. "I remember them very well."

Sabrina smiled, too. "If my parents were going to be adamant about an actual wedding, then we were adamant that it was going to be *here* and we weren't going to wait. Mother still gets all her wedding folderol, and I get to marry the man of my dreams in a few days." Her eyes suddenly glistened. "I've already told Dante that we're coming back for our first anniversary. My mother aside, this place is just magical."

Rory could do only one thing. She hugged Sabrina. "I'm glad," she said huskily.

"Everything all right here?"

Sabrina pulled back as she slid her arm through her fiancé's. "Everything's perfect." She lifted her lips for his kiss.

Immeasurably touched by Sabrina's words and maybe a little envious of the pure happiness the couple radiated, Rory looked away, giving her cheek a surreptitious swipe.

Gage, now stacking firewood next to the hearth, was watching.

He smiled slightly, and it wasn't simply shivers that danced down her spine then. Something warm and sweet and far more dangerous than mere attraction was seeping through her veins, too.

And it stayed there for the rest of the afternoon.

Even through scrubbing toilets.

"So," Megan said later that night as she sipped her spiked hot chocolate on Rory's porch. "I heard about you turning down Noah this morning."

Rory adjusted the pillow behind her in the rocking chair. The rain was more of a mist now, not strong enough to get past the covered deck. "About what?"

"The art thing with the kids."

"Oh, that. It was nothing."

"If it was nothing, you'd have agreed to free up a couple hours to play with modeling clay with them."

Rory gave Megan a look that was entirely wasted since she hadn't turned on the porch light. "I can play with modeling clay or I can cover for Frannie. I still have to keep the office going. I'm just a regular superhero. I can't do it all."

"You're a super chicken." Megan lifted her mug in a toast. "I'll give you that."

Rory huffed. But the truth of it was, she really didn't have the energy to back it up with real annoyance.

So the two of them sat there. Both cradling their mugs. Rocking chairs rocking.

"Who do you suppose that is?" Megan asked when the sound of an engine joined the soft squeak of the chair runners. Headlights were visible in the distance.

"As long as it isn't Bitsy Pith, it doesn't matter to me," Rory said. She relayed Sabrina's conversation from that morning. "What do you bet that Bitsy didn't think to check the actual weekday when she made the reservation here? She just switched the date from May of next year at her *club* to November of this year."

"At least it would explain why they arrived a day earlier—" Megan broke off when the headlights swept over the porch and stayed there as the mystery vehicle came to a stop. "I guess we know the answer now," she said under her breath when the door of the low-slung car opened and Gage stepped out.

Her friend—big help that she was—immediately offered a slyly cheerful "time to go" before she ducked her head against the damp and headed off in the dark.

Rory nervously curled her fingers over the wood rail as she watched Gage retrieve something from inside the vehicle before closing the door, switching off the interior light that had illuminated both his tall form and the wooden bird wing in the yard. "Hey," he said as he climbed the steps.

"Hey," she returned faintly. If her heart pounded any harder, it was going to jump out of her chest. She couldn't make out what he was carrying, except that it was large. "Everything all right in the main camp?"

"Far as I know. Got something for you."

"What is it?"

He laughed softly. "Maybe turn on a light and see," he suggested. "Is Killy asleep?"

"He was an hour ago." She tightened her shawl and pushed open the door, turning on both the porch light and a lamp inside. "Come on in."

She couldn't help but remember the last time he'd been there, and she slowly closed the door while he deposited his box on the coffee table.

"What is it?" she asked again.

And again, he laughed slightly. "Open and see."

Smiling a little shakily, a little uncertainly, she

unwound her shawl and dropped it on the back of the armchair before sitting on the couch in front of the plain brown box. It was definitely bigger than a breadbox.

When he sat down beside her, a fine shiver worked through her. Her gaze was skittering all over the place. From the box to his jeans-clad thigh all of six inches away from hers to the braided leather circling his wrist and back to the box again. Her hands felt unsteady as she folded back the cardboard flaps.

Then her lips parted, and her heart just melted.

It was an aquarium kit.

Her nose prickled warningly.

"Nelson deserves at least a fighting chance," he said.

She blinked hard and pressed her lips together as she worked the aquarium free. Inside the glass she could see a water test kit, filter, gravel and several varieties of plastic plants. "Where on earth did you get all this?"

"Ordered it a week ago. Drove into Wymon to pick it up this afternoon. It's just ten gallons, but it's a good starter size. Nelson will have room for a friend or two once you've got the water cycled. That'll take a couple weeks at the very least, so let's hope he sticks it out in the fishbowl long enough."

She'd been so busy that day she hadn't even realized he'd left Angel River at all. "I can't believe you did this."

He swept the cardboard carton aside. "Got these,

too." He pulled a small plastic bag from his pocket and dropped it next to the tank.

The hard candy in the bag was very distinct. "Spicy Hots," she murmured.

"Figured I still owed Killy."

She let out a garbled sound. Half a laugh. Half a sob. "'Scuse me." She launched herself from the couch and raced into the bathroom, slamming the door shut. Her hands shook as she blew her nose. Wiped her eyes. Then she looked at her reflection. Her eyes looked just as red as the tip of her nose. She yanked her ponytail tighter and dashed a quick smear of gloss over her lips.

This time, she didn't scrub it right back off.

"Rory?" Gage's voice was soft on the other side of the door. As soft as the knock he gave. "You all right?"

Her eyes burned again. She sniffed hard, squared her shoulders and opened the door.

His eyebrows were pulled together above his dark eyes. "I didn't mean to upset you."

She shook her head. "You didn't."

"That'd be more convincing, except—" He lifted his hand toward her cheek but halted just shy of it, then curled his fingers and cleared his throat. "Tears," he said abruptly.

"It's been that kind of day," she said on a choked laugh. "I can't remember the last time anyone did something so...unexpected." So sweet. So captivating.

"It's just candy and a fish tank."

She laughed again and swiped her cheek. "Killian will love it. *I* love it." Aware that they were standing in the doorway to the bathroom—reminding her of the scene she didn't want to relive—she took a step out and he shifted to one side, pushing his hands into his jacket pockets.

She ducked her chin slightly, pressing her glossed lips together as she returned to the couch. She sat and began removing the items from inside the tank only to realize that he wasn't going to also sit. And she was suddenly afraid that—now that he'd stolen half her heart so easily—he was going to drop tank and run. "You're going to show me what to do with all this, right?"

If she hadn't been watching closely, she would have missed the quick glint in his eyes. As though he was relieved. He pulled his hands free of his pockets. "Yeah." He pushed his fingers through his hair and nodded. "Sure."

She chewed the inside of her cheek to keep from smiling. Apparently even developers with employees all over the country had tender boys lurking inside.

"What do we start with first? Probably should do this in the kitchen." Thank heavens she had actually taken the time to do the dishes for once.

"Yeah. Everything needs to be rinsed off before it goes in the tank." His hands brushed hers as he took the aquarium kit from her and carried it into the kitchen.

Before long, the tank was set up, gravel, plants, water and all. "Just follow the directions and keep testing the water. Once it's ready, you can introduce Nelson to it," Gage told her as he moved the tank to a shelf that she'd cleared. "You could do it now, but it's pretty hard on fish to dump them into a tank before the nitrogen's cycled. I've done it, but—"

She leaned against the back of the armchair. "You keep fish?"

"Is it going to cement the whole nerdy image?" His smile was swift and entirely, wholly *non*-nerdy. "I think I was ten when I got my first tank. Pretty much just like this. By the time I graduated from high school, I had two fifty-gallon ones. I ended up selling both, though, 'cause Noah was a toddler and he kept wanting to dive in and play with the fishies. I was sixteen when he was born," he added as if he'd read her mind.

Which made Gage thirty-eight. Younger than she'd first thought. "Was that the end of your fish-keeping days?"

The lamplight shined on his dark hair as he looked down at the aquarium again. "I have salt-water tanks now in most of my offices. And people to keep them in perfect condition. Killian's an un-usual name."

She blinked slightly at the abrupt change of sub-ject. "Depends on your point of view. It was my mother's maiden name."

"Megan told me about her. The rapids."

"Seems Megan likes to talk more than I thought."

"Losing your mom is hard." He spoke from obvious experience.

"You, too?"

"Several years ago. Stroke."

"I'm sorry. What about your dad?"

"He died in a skiing accident when I was little."

She frowned. "Any other family?"

His lips twisted slightly. "Yeah, but that's a whole other story." He didn't elaborate.

Which naturally only increased her curiosity. "Noah's father? Were you close to him?"

He snorted softly. "Guess he told you we're half brothers. But no. I was not close to Noah's father. For that matter, neither was Noah. My mom worked for Julian for years, but they never married. Didn't even live together. He left a fortune for Noah, but that's *all* he ever did for him." He glanced at her. "She didn't marry my father, either. She wasn't traditional that way. But she did want me to watch out for Noah. He's never really been happy about that."

"Maybe he's just trying to figure out where his place is in this world. He even said it. He wants to be something that matters to someone."

"He's always mattered," Gage said quietly. Then he lifted his head, and it was as though a light had been switched off. "I don't need to keep you any longer. Stables to muck in the morning." He reached for the door and stepped outside.

She snatched up her shawl and hurried after him. "Gage, wait—"

He hesitated, but her spurt of bravery suddenly failed her. "Thanks again for everything." She moistened her lips. The gloss was long gone. "The tank and the candy." A sharp wind whipped over them, but all she did was clutch the shawl in her hands. "Not to mention everything else you've been doing. I really owe you. I know you came to learn what made us tick, but this last week has been—" She broke off, because she didn't have adequate words to describe it.

He startled her slightly when he tugged the shawl out of her grip. He shook it out and swung it around her shoulders. "I don't want you owing me anything."

Her pulse throbbed inside her head all over again, and she blamed it on the way his hands were holding the shawl together beneath her chin. "Considering everything you've been doing, that's kind of a hard thing to avoid."

The shawl grew more taut around her shoulders, as if he were reeling her in. "That's what makes this worse."

She looked up beyond that perfect mouth until she could see his eyes. "Makes what worse?" But she knew. She could feel it in every cell.

And he knew that she knew. The thumb he brushed whisper light over her chin told her so. "I made a promise." His voice was low. Deep. "That you didn't have to worry about this happening again."

"I'm more worried that it won't," she blurted, then wished the ground would just open up right then and there. Her tongue felt thick, and she looked away. "I don't know why that came out."

"But it did. And now I'm just going to have to take back that promise," he finished, his deep voice seeming to drop another octave.

It took a moment for the words to seep beyond the heartbeat clanging in her head, and when they did, everything just went still.

Her gaze slowly crept up his throat. Over his sharply angled jaw.

They never had a chance to make it to his lips, because his head was lowering toward hers. "All you have to do is say no if you—"

"No." She swallowed hard. "I mean no, I'm not going to say no."

His fingers touched her cheek. They were so, so warm. "Is that your way of saying yes?"

"Yes." It was hardly a whisper. Barely a breath.

"Good."

And then he slid his hand along her neck with just the perfect pressure and his mouth found hers.

And she was *very* glad the ground hadn't swallowed her up after all.

Chapter Twelve

The next morning, the day before Sabrina Larissa Pith and Dante Cruz Castellano would be pronounced husband and wife promptly at sunset, the sky was at last clear.

But it was freezing cold out.

Frost clung to the trees and fence posts. It coated the ground, looking almost like snow, and lent an extra crunch under Rory's boots as she pulled open the door on the hay barn.

The trio of cats inside was sleeping, their bodies pressed up against each other. Only Huey lifted his head and gave her an unwelcoming stare when she walked past them on her way to the spreader. "Good morning to you, too."

Huey blinked twice and snuggled his head back into his curled body.

"They look ambitious this morning."

She whirled around, and though she knew a goofy smile was forming, she didn't really care.

"Good morning." She watched Gage close the door and head toward her. It was the first time that week that he hadn't beaten her to the hay barn.

His eyes crinkled. "G'morning."

She almost giggled from the jittery excitement inside her. Instead, she gestured at the cats. "Really ambitious," she agreed. "Good thing we're not plagued with mice."

"Good thing."

Her gaze might as well be a fishing line reeling him in considering the way she couldn't look away from him. "I wonder where Megan is. It's not like her to be late."

"I don't really care," he said, smiling slightly. He slid an arm behind her back and pulled her close.

His lips were cold. Until they weren't.

And then, it was only a loud "ahem" that finally broke them apart.

Rory couldn't pull away, though, because if she did, Megan just might see the way her flannel shirt had come undone. So Rory rested her head against his chest and gave Megan a slit-eyed look. It was her fault for the barn door being so well oiled they hadn't even heard her entering.

The look was wasted on her friend, who was

grinning broadly. "Looks to me like the drought is finally ending." She gestured with her gloved hands. "Go ahead. Proceed. For once in my life, I think I'll go and see Bart about a chocolate croissant." And she turned on her heel and left the barn, sliding the door closed after her.

Gage's hands rubbed down Rory's arms. "The drought?"

She felt flushed. From his touch. From everything. "Megan's idea of a joke."

He laughed softly, and she was pretty certain he knew exactly what Megan had meant.

"Enticing as it would be to take advantage of the sleeping chaperones there—" he nodded to the cats, who were not giving them the time of day now "—we should probably get on with the work."

She nodded. "Probably." The fact that his maddening thumb was circling her rigid nipple brought into question what exactly he meant by "work." She angled her chin when he kissed her neck right below her ear. "But, uh, that's uh… Oh, you." She dragged his mouth to hers, luxuriating in his soft laugh as they fell back against the stacks of sweet-smelling hay.

And then his hands were delving even farther under her wool jacket, rearranging more than just her flannel shirt and slipping beneath waffle-woven thermals. She was catching her breath, gasping his name when his tongue found her nipple and his fingers found her center and she very nearly dissolved right then and there. "Wait, wait. We can't." So then why were her fingers twined in his belt loops? "I'm not on the pill."

He hesitated, his oath muffled against her breast. "And I'm not exactly packing condoms here." Suddenly, his shoulders shook, and it took her a second to realize he was laughing.

Hard. His fingers retreated from her thermals and she couldn't even protest, not really, because he kept laughing until he was positively roaring. He slid down until he was sitting on the ground, taking her right along with him.

And then she was laughing, too, and it felt so good, so wonderful, really, to just laugh and laugh until they were breathless and exhausted from it.

She leaned against him, sliding her fingers through his. "I haven't laughed like that in a long time," she finally managed. "It's almost as good as—" She broke off when he lifted their hands and kissed her knuckles.

"No," he drawled. "It's not. But that's something easily solved in time."

Her cheeks heated even as need threatened to devour her from the inside out. But she thrilled to the "in time" part.

Then he turned her hand over and kissed her palm. "Right now, we've got a crapload of stalls to clean." He stood up and tugged her to her feet. "And yes, pun intended."

Before she could even roll her eyes, he grasped

her waist and lifted her up and over the side of the spreader. "Fix your shirt," he said when he deposited her. "It's buttoned all wrong." Then he yanked a pair of work gloves from his back pocket and pulled them on.

She quickly refastened her buttons before pulling on her own work gloves. Then he started tossing up hay bales and straw, and she scooted and stacked them. "I could help you do that, you know."

He didn't even slow. "I know."

"When you made your deal with my father to learn all our secrets, was this what you had in mind?"

He grunted, and a moment later, another heavy bale landed near her feet with a fragrant puff. "When I made that deal with Sean, I didn't intend to even *be* the one who was here. Got room for a few more?"

"A few." She used her knees to push the stacks together more closely. "Who did you intend to be here?"

"Anybody else but me."

"Oh. Flattering."

His smile was long and slow. "I've learned my error." He hefted two more bales, then rested his arms on the side of the spreader. "Noah had earned himself another DUI. It should've been his last strike, but I convinced the judge to give him another shot at proving himself. That he could be responsible. That he could actually work and be a productive member of society. So I dragged him along with me, figuring I'd come up with some sort of job for him to do along the way." Gage circled her calf with his fingers almost absently. "Never thought it would be wrangling a handful of little kids for about eight hours a day. He's doing it to impress you, but the bottom line is at least he's doing it."

She shook her head. "You keep saying stuff like that, but I think you're wrong."

"Wrong that he's infatuated with you?" He squeezed her calf and smiled wryly. "Half brother or not, we've got some things in common." Then his hand slid around, and he lightly smacked her knee. "Stay there. I'll drive this thing over to the horse barn."

In seconds, he'd climbed into the cab, and the tractor engine rumbled to life. She swayed on her perch as they jerked into motion. He got out again to open the barn door when they reached it, and they rolled out into the frosty morning.

But she was blind to the wintry beauty. Instead, she was entirely rattled at the idea of Gage being infatuated with her. He hadn't said it expressly, but he might as well have.

Infatuated.

Was that what she was feeling, too? Infatuation was harmless enough, wasn't it?

But as they continued making their way around to the horse barn, all Rory could think about was fish aquariums and Spicy Hots.

* * *

She was still thinking about them thirty-six hours later, when she was sitting in the wedding barn watching Sabrina and Dante circle the dance floor.

"Dance?"

Rory glanced up at Noah and smiled. All was right with the world—except when it came to worrying that she was falling in love with Gage.

The wedding ceremony on Angel's Lookout had gone off without a hitch, the timing of Sabrina and Dante's first kiss as husband and wife perfectly co-ordinated with the golden rays of the lowering sun.

Not even Bitsy Pith could find fault.

Rory had seen enough weddings to know that the photographs would be spectacular. The subject matter was too perfect to fail.

Now, the bride and groom, their attendants, and all of the guests were here in the wedding barn, where Chef Bart's spread was on glorious display. The champagne was flowing, the music was playing and everyone—including mom- and popzilla—was dancing beneath the glittering fairy lights twined among the barn rafters.

Noah was still holding out a hopeful hand.

The last thing she wanted to do was get up on her feet and dance. The grueling week of splitting housekeeping duties with Marni was still fresh, with no end yet in sight. Rory was fairly certain she'd never scoured so many bathrooms and vacuumed so many floors in her life. The Pith group would be departing in a few days, and even though she'd worried about not having any guests for Thanksgiving week, now that they'd gotten several bookings, she longed for a break.

But she ignored her aching back and her tired feet and put her hand in Noah's, because he'd helped haul the chairs up to the lookout. Because he'd woven Bitsy's blue ribbons through the white wood so Rory could affix the floral sprays that had been delivered just in the nick of time.

For once, the children of the Pith group were actually spending time with their families and he wasn't on babysitting duty.

And her duties—until the reception concluded—were pretty much done.

"I would love to dance," she told him.

His smile was somewhere shy of brilliant, and she couldn't help but think that one day there'd come a girl who would look past that silly man bun to the sweet boy lurking inside.

He swung her around onto the dance floor, and she laughed. She wasn't really surprised that he could dance so well. She was surprised, however, that he was actually as tall as he was. He had a slighter build than Gage and she kept thinking of him as being so much smaller, but he really wasn't.

"All right," she said, "who taught you to dance?"

He looked a little chagrined. "My mother."

Her smile widened. "I love that. Maybe one day I'll be teaching Killy how to dance." Since her father had no reason to attend the wedding or reception, Killy was spending the night with him.

"Think you'll have more? Kids, I mean?"

Her gaze unerringly landed on Gage. He was standing to one side of the buffet tables in conversation with Bart, who had the whole chef thing going on, from white coat buttoned to his neck to tall toque on his head. The only point of color on Bart was the small Angel River logo emblazoned on his lapel.

Gage, on the other hand, was dressed entirely in black. The suit had undoubtedly been custom tailored. For all she knew, the shirt that fit him so perfectly had been, too. The fact that he'd packed a suit when he'd come to Angel River was surprising.

In contrast, Noah wore an ivory cashmere pullover and jeans. The man bun was there, but he'd shaved for the first time since he and Gage had arrived at the ranch, making his resemblance to his brother more pronounced.

"I never thought I'd want kids," Noah said, reminding her that she hadn't gotten around to answering his question. "Turns out they're not so bad."

"They're great," she assured him. Gage was watching them and smiling slightly. "Even when they sometimes drive you a little crazy." She remembered Gage's comment when she'd asked him if he had kids.

Thank God, no.

Had he really meant it?

Or was it just one of those things you said to

someone you didn't know when you got on a subject that you didn't want to discuss?

She was going to make herself crazy.

She dragged her gaze away and focused on Noah.
"My mom told me once that you never knew how
much you could love someone until you became a
parent. Killy is my world. But if I had another child,
I'd love him or her just as much."

"My mom used to say something like that. But I
know she preferred Gage."

"Oh, Noah. I'm sure that's not true."

"It is." He nodded, so matter-of-fact about it that
she hurt for him. "Julian—my old man—he must've
proposed to her a dozen times, but she never said
yes. She worked for him, but she wouldn't marry
him. Not even because of me."

When Gage had said Noah wasn't close to his father, either, she'd assumed that meant he hadn't been
involved in his life at all. "That doesn't mean she
preferred Gage to you. Did you *want* her to marry
your father?"

She felt the vague shrug in his shoulders. "If she
had, maybe he'd have acted more like a dad."

She thought about her ex-husband. "Marriage
isn't any guarantee of that, Noah. Not with some
people. That's not your failing, though. That was
his. And it doesn't mean he didn't love you. Maybe
it just means he didn't know how to show it."

He gave that faint shrug again. "Doesn't matter
now. He's dead."

"It'll always matter if you let it drive—" She broke off when she felt a tap on her shoulder, and she glanced around to find Marni looking unusually determined.

"Mind if I cut in?"

Delighted, Rory stepped back. Marni looked pretty as could be in a dress as bright a pink as her hair. The color in her cheeks was only slightly dimmer. "Thank you for the dance, Noah," Rory said as she surrendered her position.

With no graceful way to get out of it, he took Marni in his arms and continued dancing. He was even smiling about it when Rory chanced a look their way as she made her way around the perimeter of the room to where Gage and Bart stood. "I would say we have a success on our hands."

Bart looked over the rims of his eyeglasses. "You talking about the reception or young Marni over there?"

Rory smiled. "Maybe both."

"Thought it was supposed to be hands-off between staff and guests," Gage murmured close to her ear. Out of sight from everyone, he trailed a meaningful finger down her spine.

"Since the Piths arrived and Frannie got sick, Noah has been more like one of the crew." She sent him a look from beneath her lashes. "Same as you."

The corners of his lips twitched. "Isn't that interesting?"

"Oh, for Lord's sake," Bart said, shooing them

away. "Take it on the dance floor or something. I'm too old for all the pheromones flying between you."

Gage wrapped her hand in his. "An excellent idea." He drew her toward the edge of the crowd and pulled her close even though the beat of the music was fast.

She didn't care. There were enough other people dancing that the two of them were barely noticeable. And she wasn't giving her sore feet a single thought. Not when she could feel his long fingers splayed against the small of her back the way they were.

"Pretty dress," he murmured. "Thought it was bad form to outshine the bride."

"It'd take the sun to outshine Sabrina," Rory returned. The girl was radiant with happiness. "But I appreciate the compliment all the same. You clean up pretty well yourself. I've been meaning to ask all night. Do you always travel with a suit?"

He chuckled. "Regrettably. Old habits die hard. Was talking to Ludo earlier."

"The wedding photographer?"

"Ludovico Bianchi is a master wedding photo-*journalist*, sweetheart. He doesn't pose the shots. He records—"

"—the truth and realism in the moment," she finished, trying not to get too flustered by the *sweetheart*. "I know the gist."

"Then you shouldn't be surprised to hear he wants to do a story on Angel River."

She pulled her head back from the spot against

his jaw where it naturally fit to give him a narrow look. "How do you know that?"

"How do you think? He told me. You should agree and get a tease of his story to push the flash deal. Bitsy Pith might be a pain in your beautiful derriere—" his fingers dipped an inch lower on her spine "—but she didn't stint when it came to hiring him. His work's well-known."

Rory arched back, reaching around to catch his hand before it could drop farther. "Stop," she whispered fiercely. "Someone's going to notice."

"Then let's go where nobody can see."

She was so sorely tempted she was quaking inside. He had no idea of the gift that Megan had slipped into Rory's hand while the reception was gearing up. But Rory did, and she'd been swamped with anticipation of this moment ever since. "I can't just disappear at a function like this," she reminded herself as much as him.

"Then when?"

"After!"

"This thing could go on all night. As Noah keeps telling me, I'm not a young man anymore. I could have a heart attack waiting—"

She laughed, covering his mouth with her hand. "You're a nut." Then she twisted out of his arms. "And it won't last all night, because they only have the band and the bartending team until midnight. But let me get my coat. We'll go out and... I don't know. Take a stroll." She gave him a stern glance. "*Just* a stroll." And maybe the cold air would cool them both off.

The air was cold, for sure. But it didn't cool Gage off all that much.

And it quickly became apparent that they weren't the only ones out for a little "stroll." They even happened upon a couple making out in one of the boats tied near the bridge.

Still, the few kisses Gage did manage to steal were enough to keep him going through the rest of the interminably long wedding reception.

But finally, it was last call. Most of the guests who had kids had called it a night once the bride and groom had cut the cake earlier in the evening. But that still left a good-size crowd cozying up to the bar for that last drink of the night before they climbed into the vans to be shuttled by Megan and Marni back to the Uptown camp. Meanwhile, the band was packing up their equipment and loading it in their truck. Like the bartending team and the couple of servers Rory had hired, they had a longer drive ahead of them than just the few miles to Uptown. They had to return all the way to Wymon.

Gage and Noah helped Bart break down the buffet and pack it all to go back to the lodge while Rory went around collecting flowers and linens and doing pretty much everything else that still needed doing.

He knew she was exhausted, but she kept on going.

He wasn't sure he'd ever met anyone who worked as hard as she did. And coming from him, that was saying a lot.

She'd kicked off the sexy high heels she'd been wearing earlier, and her long, narrow sheath of a dress swished against the wood floor as she walked back and forth collecting this, sorting that. She'd done something with her hair for the wedding, too. She usually wore it loose or pulled back in a ponytail. But tonight she'd twisted it up in a thick, coiling rope. It emphasized the slender column of her neck.

And he'd been thinking about letting that coil down for nearly eight hours.

He shot Bart a look. Even the chef had let his hair down at this point—at least he'd doffed the toque and loosened a few buttons on his white coat. "You're not doing something obscene like baking bread in a few hours, are you?"

Bart chuckled. "Not this week. It's no-knead bread this week." He snapped a lid down on the last plastic tub. "Plus we have that special post-wedding brunch to deal with tomorrow. Guess that'd be *today.* Fortunately, everything is set to go for that. I'll just be carving beef and making omelets on the fly."

Noah reached for the tub and hefted it up. "Does *every* wedding go like this?"

"Eh." Bart waved his hand. "More or less. Under the skin, you know, it's all pretty much the same stuff." He picked up a big trash bag that Rory had filled with the table linens to be washed and followed Noah out to the UTV he was using.

Rory dropped an armload of ivory flowers on the table in front of him.

"What happens with all of the flowers?"

"Bitsy only wanted these for the reception." She moved her shoulders slightly as she stroked one of the ruffled petals. She gave Gage a wry look. "She has *other* decor in mind for the brunch. That'll be all blues and yellows. Instead of blues and—" she lifted an encompassing arm "—ivory."

"What was up at the lookout?" He hadn't gone over for the ceremony. One, the place had barely enough room for all of the wedding party and guests, and, two, he'd been down here helping Bart transport all the last-minute food from the ovens at the lodge. Because, as nice a setup as the wedding barn was—and Gage had to admit it had a particularly appealing location on the other side of the river away from the lodge—it did not have its own kitchen.

He needed to remember to mention that point to April and Jed. In case they wanted something similar at the Rad.

But right now, his mind kept short-circuiting at the way Rory's fingertip stroked over that velvety flower.

"More peonies like these," she said. "Just none of the blue ribbons." Her arm cut a swath through the air. "That had to be all white. Pure. For the ceremony, of course. The only blue allowed was the programs."

"That you printed and folded."

"Megan and Marni helped." She smiled wearily. "I think I probably bought out all the peonies this side of California just to have enough. Poor Bitsy. She had a spring wedding in her mind that landed squarely in November."

"Poor Bitsy nothing." He'd watched Rory already fill five giant trash bags with just flowers. "Got enough there to make a bed of them." As soon as the words came out, that was the vision that filled his head.

Laying Rory down on a thick white cushion of flowers. Pulling away a shimmering white veil from her head.

He yanked at his tie, loosening it enough to free the button at his neck. He was more tired than he thought if he was imagining *that*.

"I do love them," she said. Then she looked at him, humor lighting her blue eyes. "Compost pile is going to smell really pretty for a while." She shook open another black bag and, with one long sweep across the table, sent flowers tumbling down into it.

Then she propped her hands on her hips and looked around them. "I think that's it."

Sure enough, all of the tables were bare, the chairs tucked in, the decorations gone.

"We don't have anything else going on down here

now, so maybe the floors can wait to be mopped until Frannie is back." She pushed her feet into her shoes with a little groan. "Oh, for a good foot massage."

He dropped her coat around her shoulders. It was a stylish thing. Long and black and fitted. Entirely different from that muddy red one she wore nearly every day. "You need more help."

She sent him a wry smile as they headed for the door. "So I keep hearing."

Then she hit the lights on the way out, plunging the cavernous interior into black.

The UTV with the trailer was gone. Bart and Noah had taken it across to the lodge already. Gage nudged Rory into the last one remaining, stuffed the flower bags in the cargo box as well as he could, then climbed behind the wheel himself. With the cold weather enclosure in place, it seemed smaller inside.

She let out a soft sigh, her shoulder leaning into his as he started driving back. When he crossed the narrow bridge spanning the river, her palm seemed to naturally come to rest on his thigh.

His own tiredness fled. "Do you need to stop at the lodge?"

She made another soft sound. He felt her shake her head.

When he reached the loop road, instead of heading toward the building on the knoll, he kept right on going, and he didn't stop until he reached her cabin.

By then, she was a limp weight against his side. She'd fallen asleep.

He sat there for a moment, staring out at the star-speckled sky while he willed his body to calm the hell down. It probably was just as well. He hadn't had a condom the other morning in the barn. He hadn't had a single opportunity to acquire one in the time since.

He was pretty sure the universe was having a hell of a laugh at his expense.

He carefully slid her over so he could get out of the utility vehicle without disturbing her and went up to check the cabin door. It swung open when he turned the knob, which was convenient for the moment but still made him want to lecture her about common safety. He left the door open and returned to the UTV. He started to reach for her but hesitated.

Suddenly coming to a decision, he worked a couple of the bags free from the cargo box and carried them inside her cabin. She'd left a lamp on by the aquarium being prepared for Nelson, so he had no trouble seeing his way up the stairs. Once he reached the landing, the night-light plugged into the wall helped the rest of the way. The cabin had the same floor plan as where he and his brother were staying. Distinguishing Killy's room from Rory's even in the faint light was a no-brainer.

Feeling a little strange because he'd never once done anything remotely like this, he turned on the small lamp on her nightstand, then folded back the

his tie, putting his knee on the side of the bed before kissing her.

He was hard and she was wet, and the one portion of his mind still capable of thought after he finally buried himself inside her and swallowed her gasping cries was that he owed Megan.

Big-time.

It was a long while later before either one of them had the strength to speak. Rory's fingers were trailing over his bare hip, her silky leg gliding along his. Her uncoiled hair streamed over his chest.

"Have to say—" there was a smile in her soft, husky voice "—when you give a girl flowers, you really give a girl flowers."

Chapter Thirteen

*B*liss.

There was no other word to describe what it felt like waking in Gage's arms.

The few flowers they hadn't already dislodged from the bed quickly ended up on the floor when he smiled sleepily and pulled her down to him once more.

By the time they made their way to the lodge to set up for Bitsy Pith's big post-wedding brunch, Rory knew she'd never been so well loved.

From the soles of her feet that he'd rubbed while he kissed his way up her legs, to the tears he'd brushed away from the corners of her eyes when her pleasure grew too great, there wasn't one inch of her that Gage hadn't discovered.

One day, perhaps, she'd tell Megan about waking up on a cushion of flowers.

She owed her that much, at least, for having slid those two packets into Rory's hand during the wedding reception.

But for now, she was going to hold the experience close—because it was in that moment she'd realized she was falling head over heels in love with Gage.

She knew perfectly well that it couldn't last.

How could it, when her life was at Angel River and Gage's wasn't?

He wasn't going to stay there forever. He had a business to run. A life that was entirely separate from hers waited for him.

But until then, Rory was going to savor every moment.

That didn't mean, however, that she wanted to advertise this new development in their relationship to everyone. "I have Killy to consider," she told Gage as they went in through the storeroom of the lodge.

"I get it." He wrapped his arms around her waist, pulling her up tight against him. "I have the kid in my place to consider, too."

"Noah's not a kid," she murmured against his kiss. "And he's been a huge help—" She broke off when his hand slid between her thighs. She frantically pulled at his wrist even though everything inside her yearned to follow the press of his palm. "We *can't*. Not here!"

He laughed softly. "But I love the way you come

so sweet and—" He swiftly released her when the hinges of the door to the kitchen squeaked, and he walked right past Bart with a calm "g'morning" that gave no hint of what the chef had nearly interrupted.

Rory, on the other hand, was left in a flush of wanting that plagued her the rest of the day and bloomed with fresh heat every time Gage's eyes caught hers.

He knew it, too.

Fortunately, the brunch was a raving success. She even caught Bitsy genuinely smiling as she made her way among her guests. Then Rory's dad arrived with Killy in tow as half the guests joined in a game of touch football and the other half headed for the river and the rowboats.

Even though the wedding was finally over, that didn't mean the guest rooms and cabins didn't need tending.

"I'll make you pay for this," she murmured to Gage as she passed him with her arms full of sheets from Uptown.

"I'm looking forward to it," he murmured as he headed the other way with an armload of firewood.

The payment, however, had to wait. Luckily, the rest of the day passed quickly. Then the next morning, after a mass exodus that was far more orderly than the group's premature arrival, all of Uptown was finally quiet once more.

The lodge was empty, too.

The only guest cabin being occupied was the Brown.

The lull wouldn't last forever, not with more guests coming in the following week for the Thanksgiving holiday. But it was enough to give them all a much-needed rest as they regrouped.

And Rory, taking advantage of the fact that Killy was at school, her dad and Bart were in Wymon, and Marni had wrangled Noah and Megan into helping her repaint the kitchen in her cabin, finally had her chance to extract payment.

She picked up Gage in one of the UTVs and could tell by his expression as they headed toward the staff cabins that he figured they were heading to hers. But when she kept driving right on past, his certainty turned to curiosity. "Where are we going?"

She slid him a smile. "You'll see."

She was more nervous than she let on. It had been so long since she'd been up to the studio. She could well find it infested with displaced barn mice.

Hardly ideal for the tryst she had in mind.

But when the UTV made it through the trail overgrown from disuse and she pulled to a stop in front of the small square building, the look in Gage's eyes more than made up for any nervousness she felt.

He helped her pull the riotous shrubs away from the windows and the door. She'd never had a reason to lock it, and when she turned the knob, it opened easily.

Inside, the windows that faced the same view

he'd seen the first time he'd kissed her were caked with dust. Otherwise, the interior looked the same as it always had. Shelves loaded with supplies and tools. Two different kilns. Her wheel still sat near the window, because she'd liked looking out as she'd worked.

Gage's hand curved over her shoulder. "How'd you learn to carve wood with the chain saw?"

"I did some ice carving when I lived in Seattle. Never did much with wood at all." She kissed his hand and moved farther into the studio. "Place is cleaner than I expected." She noticed his expression. "What?"

"You amaze me."

She flushed slightly. "I can't imagine why."

"You created that *wing* without endless practice? Jesus, Rory. What would you be able to create if you could focus on your art?"

"It doesn't really matter." She picked up a wrapped piece of clay. It had gone hard and dry. "I don't have time for all of this anymore, anyway." She dropped it back onto the plaster-topped wedging table. "Not with the ranch."

"Do they have to be mutually exclusive?"

"Yes," she admitted. "I was never good at splitting my concentration when it comes to this." She waved her arm, encompassing the studio and all that it contained. "If I'm running Angel River, I have to run it. I can't be thinking about which clay bodies I prefer and whether I can coax more color from a glaze if I just try one more combination." She didn't even realize she had tears in her eyes until one spilled hot onto her cheek.

She dashed it away and moved to the larger of the kilns. "Can you imagine how much worse things would be for the ranch if I didn't keep my focus where it belonged?" She restlessly lifted the lid. Three honey pots sat inside, still unfinished. She closed the lid again and glanced at him.

His gaze was warm on her face, as if he saw everything that she wasn't saying. Her throat tightened even more.

"The art is not worth the price that keeps coming with it," she admitted huskily.

"Your mom didn't die because you were away living *your life*," he said quietly. "Your dad didn't get sick because you were throwing pots."

She ran her finger around the edge of her potter's wheel. "Megan tell you that, too?"

"Educated guess." He crossed to her and kissed the top of her head, sliding his arms around her. "Hire another manager. Come with me to Denver."

She froze, yet everything inside her was wildly spinning. "What?"

"You and Killy." He turned her around to face him. "He can get the advanced placement he needs without having to go to a school fifty miles away." He smiled slightly. "You can have a studio with all the clay and chain saws you've ever wanted."

She swallowed hard. "I...I don't know what to

say." She wasn't even certain exactly what he was asking.

"Say yes. And I'll take care of the rest." Then he let out an impatient sigh and yanked his cell phone from his jacket pocket. "Archer. My lawyer. Impeccable timing as usual." He silenced the vibrating and tucked the phone away again. "Come to Denver."

He said it so easily. As if it weren't the least bit momentous. "Wh-where would we live?"

His eyes searched hers. "Where do you want to live?"

She could hardly breathe. "Gage—"

"With me." He cupped her face in his hands. "Where did you think I meant?"

"I don't know." She swallowed. "This is all happening too fast. I can't think straight."

"Sometimes thinking is overrated. Sometimes you have to go with your gut. And mine tells me the world needs more beauty, courtesy of Rory McAdams." He brushed his lips over hers. "And I need more of her nights."

"This is not what I came up here for," she said faintly.

Suddenly, his eyes held fresh intent. "What *did* you come up here for?"

Despite the uncertainties and temptation whirling dizzily inside her, heat streaked through her veins. "You know very well what for. To torture you for that business in the storeroom yesterday."

His lips curved. "Torture me?" He reached around

her and picked up the coiled cutoff wire she'd used to slice clay and let it dangle from one of the small wooden end rods. "Not planning to garrote me, are you?"

"I was thinking more along the lines of this." She tossed aside the tool and drew his hand to the juncture of her thighs.

His eyes darkened as his fingers cupped her through her jeans. "Aren't you suddenly the bold one?"

"Yes." Her legs were already going weak.

His head lowered toward hers, his breath whispering over her ear. "If you're really bold, unzip your pants."

Her hands shook. She unzipped her jeans. Then moaned inadvertently when his hand slid beneath her panties.

He inhaled on a hiss when he found her. "How." His fingers slowly delved. Swirled through her wetness. "How is this torturing me?"

She leaned against the wedging table, her head falling back as she watched him from beneath her lashes. Her breath was already coming harder, and she could feel her nerves coiling. Tightening. Her fingers curled against the cold plaster at either side of her. "Because I don't have a third little packet," she breathed shakily. "And I don't think you've all of a sudden conjured one, either."

And for some reason, she'd stupidly thought that particular fact would be harder on him than on her.

The corner of his lips lifted, and his eyes darkened even more. "Then by all means…" His fingers slid farther, pressed deeper and she was suddenly gasping, convulsing. Before the tremors even had a chance to abate, he'd swept her jeans away and lifted her onto the table, his head lowering to join his hands. "Let me be *really* tortured."

She was the one who cried out for mercy, though.

He just laughed softly, exultantly, and "suffered" some more.

Gage didn't say anything more about her moving to Denver, but as the month dwindled—taking Thanksgiving along with it—his words never left her thoughts.

Now it was December, and the end of Gage's stay was drawing even closer.

The flash sale—helped by the spectacular photography of Ludovico Bianchi—turned out to be a wild success.

Even though there was no snow yet, they had more three-night reservations than Rory could recall ever having before.

Noah and Gage helped them haul the enormous white spruce her dad had ordered from a local tree farm into the lodge. It stood almost as tall as the exposed beams in the ceiling, and all of the Angel River staff—even Seth and Toonie—helped decorate it. They fastened fresh boughs of greenery and red ribbons on the staircase banisters. They hung mistletoe in doorways and twirled lights around the railings outside. Holiday carols played on the sound system nearly twenty-four hours a day.

When it came to ambience, Angel River had it in spades. Of course, the food and booze had never been a problem, and while it remained to be seen if the flurry of new business could sustain itself, Rory couldn't help but feel hopeful.

Thankfully, Frannie was fully recuperated from her bout with the chicken pox by the time the first of the holiday guests began checking into the lodge. Rory was so grateful she was back to work, she gave Frannie the promotion to head of housekeeping and told her to hire someone to help her. Maybe, like Noah had with the children from the wedding, Frannie just needed a reason to rise to the occasion.

There was no denying the woman seemed to show a brand-new commitment to the work.

And yet more days dwindled away, giving Gage and Rory precious little time to sneak away when nobody was looking. She knew they hadn't fooled Megan, of course. And not Bart, either. But Killy remained innocently unaware of his mother's secret and so, apparently, was Noah, who'd been spending more and more time with Marni anyway.

By the second weekend in December, nearly every room in the lodge was booked.

Instead of the huge bonfire down by the river, they kept one going in the firepit outside the lodge and served gallons of Rory's hot chocolate at the mahogany bar.

She was refilling the bowls of toppings—marshmallows and caramels were neck and neck when it came to favorites—and watching Noah across the room sitting at the grand piano she'd rented from a place in Montana, when Gage came up next to her. He secretly brushed his hand over hers before he filled a mug with the rich cocoa.

"Did you know Noah played?"

"He took lessons when he was little. But otherwise?" He shook his head.

"What else did he do when he was little? Besides dive for fishies in your aquariums?"

Gage smiled wryly. "He was a holy terror. My mother said he was just like me." His smile turned bittersweet. "Then he got a little older. I was out on my own. Things changed."

She squeezed his hand. "Things can change again."

"Probably not that much." The big door opened, letting in a group of laughing people, and they both automatically glanced that way.

Then Gage let out a surprised grunt, and he suddenly crossed toward the group, his hand outstretched. "Why the hell didn't you say you were coming?"

She watched him clasp hands with a tall blond guy then swing a woman with wildly curling brown hair around in a circle.

Rory couldn't help smiling as he drew the couple toward her.

"—and so we thought, why not," the woman was saying. "It's not that long a drive from Braden. And this is our last free weekend of the year."

"Didn't expect to see this many people here," the man added. "Thought it'd be a good surprise, but the surprise'll be on us if there's no room at the inn."

"There's room," Gage assured him. He briefly dropped his hand on Rory's shoulder. "This is Rory McAdams. She runs the place. Honey, this is my lawyer, Archer Templeton, and his much prettier better half, Nell."

"I'm almost his better half," Nell said with a laugh. "The wedding's still a few weeks off. New Year's Eve." She clasped Rory's hand in both of hers. "It's so nice to meet you. Gage has told us so much about you."

Rory's eyebrows rose as she gave Gage a look. "Has he?"

"Well, about Angel River," the other woman allowed with another laugh. She pulled off her black swing coat, and Rory realized she was pregnant. "It's so beautiful here. The pictures I saw don't do it justice."

Archer took her coat and added it to his own over his arm. He looked from Gage to Rory. "Seriously. *Is* there a room?"

"There's almost always a room at this inn," she answered wryly. "Here. Let me take those." She reached for the coats. "I'll go and get your room key."

He reached into his pocket. "Can I just give you the credit card?"

She waved it away. "Please. You're Gage's friend. Consider it Angel River's pleasure." She swung her arm wide, taking in the festive room all around them. "Make yourselves at home." With coats in hand, she quickly started out of the great room, stopping off to hang the coats on hooks before heading for the office.

Gage watched her go, then slid Archer a look. "What's really going on? You didn't say anything about wanting to come up here last time we talked." Which had been damn near every day about one thing or another, including the wedding from which Gage still hadn't managed to extricate himself. He'd become resigned at this point. Just because he'd be surrounded by a bunch of people named Templeton didn't have to mean anything. Thanks to the fact that his mother had never married his father, his name had always been Stanton.

"I could ask the same question," Archer countered. *"Honey?"*

Gage eyed him blankly.

"Interesting," Archer said, giving Nell a look.

"You gonna keep talking in code or what?"

Archer's smile widened. "We came up here because we wanted to give the news in person." He leaned forward conspiratorially. "All of Rambling

Mountain that you don't own is officially on the fast track to become Wyoming's newest state park. The first one to be named in decades."

Nell was practically bouncing on her toes. "He found out just this morning," she added. "We stopped long enough to tell April and Jed."

Gage couldn't help staring. "A state park. They're actually going for it."

"A press release is going out from the Parks Department sometime next week," Archer told him. "It'll still take time before all is said and done. First thing that'll go up is a ranger station while the access road to the lake is built. Other plans are still in the talking stage. But yeah. They're actually going for it. So congratulations. Once the Rad is up and running as a guest ranch, it'll be bordered by land that people are going to line up to experience. There's no way the Rad could fail."

They'd been working toward this for months, and now that it was happening, it felt strangely surreal. "Guess we should celebrate with something more than hot chocolate." Gage went behind the bar and set up a couple glasses.

Nell patted her small baby bulge. "I'll stick with the hot chocolate. Which—" she peered over the array of accompaniments "—is pretty impressive." She gave Archer a look. "What do you think Vivian would say to having a hot chocolate bar at the wedding?"

Archer laughed. "Since you have my grandmother wrapped around your finger, is that really a question?" He took the shot of bourbon that Gage handed him. He waited until Gage had his own, then tapped his glass to it. "Congrats again, man. The Stanton magic strikes again."

Gage chuckled, aware of Rory heading their way once more, though a portion of his attention was still on the hand Nell was still pressing against her belly.

He felt a little buzzing inside his head.

With only one exception, he and Rory had been scrupulously careful to use protection.

She still hadn't answered him about Denver. If she were to get pregnant, would she then?

"Here." Rory handed Archer a small envelope containing the card key when she reached them. "I've put you in the baron's suite. It has one of the best views on the property."

"Top of the stairs and end of the hall," Gage added. "Helluva bathroom."

Rory's cheeks pinkened. Because he'd cornered her there just a few weeks earlier when she'd been cleaning the vacated suite. They'd had a truly exceptional time together under the shower spray.

The miraculous part was nobody even noticed that she'd spent part of the afternoon with wet hair and a glow on her face.

And now, all he could do was probe that buzzing inside his head. He wanted Rory and Killy with him in Denver.

But was he really ready for all the rest, especially when Gage knew that when it came to life outside of business, his record was anything but magical?

Chapter Fourteen

The brunch that Bart had put on for the Pith group had been so popular they decided to begin regularly offering it on Sundays, at least for as long as the flash deal kept bringing in new people.

Rory's dad and Killy came down and joined her for the first one. It was the first time in a long while that the three of them had a meal together in the lodge. All the other tables scattered throughout the great room were occupied as well. Only a few guests were hearty enough to brave sitting outside on the deck, even with the propane heaters running.

Gage was one of them; he was sitting at a table visiting with a couple who'd come in from Chicago.

His lawyer had left a week ago, staying only the one night even though Rory had assured them they were welcome to stay for the whole weekend in the suite. But Nell had said they needed to get back. Both she and Archer had given her unexpected hugs on the way out. It was so obvious that Gage and Archer were good friends, she'd teased him later about the way he only ever referred to the man as his lawyer.

"He *is* my lawyer," he'd countered lazily and returned his attention to kissing his way to her breasts. They'd had a whole thirty minutes together behind the locked door of her office before duty had called again in the form of new arrivals.

They hadn't had another opportunity for locked doors until last night, when Killy spent his usual Saturday night with her dad.

"Can I have more fruit?" Killy's question dragged her from her thoughts.

"I'll get it for you." He still hadn't learned the art of not touching every piece of fruit whether he intended eating it or not. "Dad, you want anything?"

"I'm good." He was working a crossword puzzle from a three-day-old newspaper and barely glanced up.

She went over to the buffet, where Megan was making a process out of selecting one of Bart's handmade bagels, and picked up a plate.

Her friend gave her an arch look. "Anything new?"

Rory dropped a spoonful of sliced berries on the plate. "I'm not pregnant," she said under her breath.

She'd had to tell Megan about her and Gage's slip. Strangely, she had not told her about Denver. She wasn't sure why.

"Too bad."

"Megan!"

Her friend shrugged unrepentantly. "You make good babies. I was right about the three weeks. I'm right about this."

Rory glanced at the deck beyond the glass-paned doors.

"Right about what?" Noah reached past them to grab a carafe of fresh-squeezed orange juice.

"Nothing," Rory said quickly while Megan muffled a laugh.

He gave them both suspicious looks but walked away again, taking the carafe with him.

"They look cute together, don't they?" Megan nodded toward the table he was aiming for out on the deck, where Marni was sitting. "Man Bun and Pinkie."

"You really need to stop giving everyone nicknames," Rory scolded. Though she had to agree, Noah and Marni together did cut a striking pair. She rotated a tiny ceramic Christmas tree to better show off the even tinier red bulbs on it. "Have you given *them* a three-week timeline?"

Megan just laughed, and Rory brought the plate of fruit over to Killy. She jiggled his wannabe man bun. "We're having Donna cut this next week," she warned.

He shrugged, clearly more interested in the fruit he was shoveling into his mouth. As soon as he finished, he asked if he could go outside.

She saw no reason he couldn't. "Take your coat."

He grabbed it off the spare chair and pulled it on as he ran out to the deck, where Noah and Marni were sitting.

Rory slid onto Killy's vacated chair. "Feeling all right, Dad?"

He looked up at her. "Any reason why I wouldn't be?" Then he sighed and pushed aside his crossword. "Honey, you have to stop worrying about me."

"Might as well ask me to jump in the river." Her gaze strayed toward the deck again. "You should think about taking a vacation," she said. "Go somewhere warm. Play golf."

"What for? I hate golf." He refolded his newspaper and slid it toward her. "New state park is coming."

Faint dismay whisked across her nerves as she pulled the paper closer. A black-and-white photo of the peaks of Rambling Mountain was accompanied by a smaller one of a wizened old man. "Landowner Leaves Mountain for State," the headline read. A few lines of print beneath it comprised the entire article.

"Going to be one of the next hot spots in the state," her dad said. Needlessly.

Gage had to know. The paper was days old. His *attorney* had been there just a week ago.

Yet he hadn't told her.

"Excuse me." She left the table and went out onto the deck. As soon as she did, the chill permeated the knit of her turtleneck. She caught Gage's eye and he followed her when she reentered the lodge, neither of them stopping until they'd reached the office.

She'd barely closed the door when he was reaching for her, and even though she wanted to succumb, she sidled away and moved to sit behind her desk.

His brows jerked together slightly. "What?"

She folded her hands over her desk pad and the doodles there. "Hear there's going to be a new state park. On land surrounding the guest ranch that you're planning."

His dark gaze was steady. "Yes."

"And you didn't say anything about it."

"We've all been pretty busy around here. You most of all."

He was right, but that still didn't soothe the little churning that had started inside her. "You must be pleased about it, though. It's almost a guarantee you'll be successful right out of the gate."

"Yeah, but it's obviously bugging you."

"What's *bugging* me is the fact that you didn't say anything about the land becoming a state park! You know it's bound to have a greater effect on our business here at Angel River!"

"What's affecting Angel River is that you're afraid to get someone in here qualified to run the place and move on with your life!"

She lifted her chin. "Good to know you've gained

all the expertise you need. Not just about Angel River, but about me as well."

"This isn't about the state park," he said flatly. "This is about what's going on between *us*."

"No," she said doggedly, "this is about *your* business competing against *my* business."

He let out an abrupt laugh. "Sweetheart, that is no competition."

He was right. Again. Stanton Development was huge. Even with their surge in business—which she could only attribute to him since it had been his idea—Angel River was just…Angel River. And their hopes of competing against a brand-new property bordering a brand-new, unexplored state park were slim. "Then I'm surprised you wasted so much time here learning the secrets of our success, when it clearly wasn't even necessary!"

"I told you—" He broke off, starting to look annoyed. He took a breath and started fresh. "I told you I needed a place to get Noah away from everything. Angel River was just…convenient." He shoved back his hair. "And getting involved with you—"

"Was what?" She shot out of her chair, and it bounced against the credenza. "Another convenience?" Right about then, she felt as out of control as Bitsy Pith.

"For God's sake, Rory. You know that's not true. When, *when* haven't I been clear that the two of us sleeping together has *nothing* to do with business?" His voice rose, and his hand sliced the air. "You're freaking out because I asked you to come back with me to Denver! And you're either too afraid to admit you want to or too afraid to just tell me no!"

They both jerked at the sound from the doorway.

Noah stood there holding a brightly colored gift bag with tissue sticking out the top. His face was pale, and his blue eyes blazed. "Bastard." He pitched the bag to one side as he advanced, and it hit the coffee table with an ominous sound of glass breaking. "You just had to do it, didn't you? You had to steal the one thing you knew I wanted and—"

Gage swore. "Grow up, Noah. Not everything in this world is about you!"

"No. It's all about Gage Stanton! The perfect son," Noah spat. "The one whose touch turns everything to gold." His curled fist suddenly flew. "Except you don't know sh—"

Rory cried out, dashing out from behind her desk.

Gage, though, had deflected his brother's swing and held a tight, hard grip on his brother's arm. "I know you're still a kid playing at being a man." Looking disgusted, he shoved at Noah, releasing him, and his brother stumbled back.

Noah, though, caught his footing and looked like a bull ready to charge again.

"Stop it!" Heedless, she ran between them, her arms outstretched. "Stop it right now!"

"Dammit, Rory." Gage reached for her, trying to push her to one side. "Get out of the way before you get hurt."

She slapped his hands away. "The only ones who're going to get hurt are the both of you!"

She shoved Noah's shoulder before he could butt Gage. "If you're gonna behave like idiots, you can do it somewhere else!" She pushed at the younger man one more time for good measure. "Now *get* over there," she snarled, pointing behind him. And though he didn't exactly slink away in shame, he did at least back off a foot. "I am very fond of you, Noah, but nobody has *stolen* anything. Especially me." Her hands were shaking when she raked back her hair. "You know I don't feel that way about you, and if you were honest, you'd know you don't feel that way about me! I'm just someone who listens to you! And *you*." She turned her wrath on Gage. "The only thing I am *afraid* of is falling all over again for someone who can't tell the truth!"

His teeth clenched. "I told you. The state park thing has *nothing* to do with us."

"And it never will!" She swatted the air. "*How* can you behave like this with your own brother?"

His head jerked back. "What?"

"Family is everything." She stuck her face close to his. "Ev-er-y-*thing*!"

Noah snorted behind her. "Gage doesn't care about family. He cares about controlling the money Julian left me." He lifted his hands and wriggled his fingers like he was playing with marionettes. "He cares about making sure we're all dancing to his tune." He dropped his hands. "If he cared about family, he'd tell some of them that he actually *exists*!"

She saw the pallor creep into Gage's face. "What's he mean?"

But Gage wasn't listening to her. He was staring at his brother. "What do you know about that?"

Noah sneered. "That you're Thatcher Templeton's son? Vivian Templeton's *grandson*? The old lady's worth ten times what Julian was. I'm just surprised you haven't spoken up so you can get your claws in that particular pot at the end of the rainbow."

Gage sank bank on the edge of the desk. "How'd you know?"

"You're not the only one who had Althea Stanton for a mom," Noah reminded him. "Just 'cause she loved you more didn't mean she never told me about *your* father. *Thatcher*." He puffed his fingers out in a little explosion. "About how he was estranged from his wealthy, wealthy mama. How she never knew about the two of them. Or about you." His whole body jerked with emphasis. "My mother could work for Julian. Sleep with him and have me. But nobody was ever going to replace *Thatcher*. Father of the sainted Gage." Noah looked at Rory. His eyes gleamed. "Imagine what it would do for that old woman to learn her firstborn had produced a son before he died."

Rory looked at Gage. "Templeton. As in Archer? Your *lawyer*? The one you won't even call a friend? Is he a relative, too?"

His compressed lips were nearly bloodless. His silence was stony.

"I don't know you at all." She turned on her heel and walked out of the office. But the truth was inside her head, mocking her with every step.

Of course she knew him. She just hadn't paid attention. *Relationships don't work for me.* He'd said so himself. Work was the only thing that suited him. He'd never claimed to love her. In asking her to go with him to Denver, he hadn't been offering a lifelong commitment.

She could hear the laughter and voices as she neared the great room, and she stopped. She didn't have the stomach to play her Angel River part just then.

She turned on her heel and went back to her office.

The two men were still there squared off against each other, but at least they didn't look as though they were a breath away from throwing punches. She wrapped her hand around the doorknob. "This is my office." The words sounded as harsh as they tasted. "Get out."

Noah was the first to go, though the look he sent Gage was searing as he brushed past her and left.

She looked to Gage, tightening her hand on the doorknob and ignoring her shakiness inside as she stared him down. If he thought she'd fold first, he had another think coming.

But he didn't make it easy.

Finally though, he pushed away from the edge of the desk and walked out.

She slammed the door shut so hard that one of the framed awards fell off the wall and broke when it landed.

Then she sniffled and sank down on the couch.

She picked up the gift bag that Noah had thrown. It was heavy, and she was half-afraid to read the tag on it. But it wasn't from him. The handwriting was girlish. Looping. "To our Angel River family," the tag said.

It was from Sabrina and Dante.

Remorse joined the rest of the funereal feelings churning inside her. She carefully lifted the tissue, bringing with it a glass figurine of a winged angel.

Broken in two.

"Her mother used to have a temper," Sean said. He set a bottle of whiskey and three short glasses on the table between Gage and Noah and sat down, looking out from the deck toward the glimmering blue river. A group of guests was on foot, clearly heading that way. Closer by, Gage could see Killy and Damon running around, tossing a football between them.

"Fierce," Sean added. "When Eleanor got going, it was always a good idea to just let the storm blow over." He chucked the collar of his coat up his neck before unscrewing the bottle. "She liked to smash a dish now and again." He poured a shot into each glass. "Never around the guests, of course."

Gage looked from the amber liquid to the older man, wondering what he was up to. He knew Noah couldn't—shouldn't—drink. But Sean's gaze was distant. Clearly stuck in his reminiscence.

As for Noah, his expression was stoic.

Though Gage couldn't explain why, for the better part of an hour, they'd both been sitting at opposite sides of the table without throwing a punch. Ever since Rory had thrown them out of her office.

Instead of heading to opposite sides of the earth, there they were.

It made as much sense as anything else.

Sean lifted one of the glasses. "To the women it's our privilege to love and our challenge to understand." He smiled faintly and tossed back the contents.

Then he got up and began heading toward the door.

Noah suddenly stirred. "Who *did* she smash the dishes around, then?" He looked over his shoulder at Sean.

Sean's lips twitched. "Only the people she loved, of course." He went inside. Several minutes later, he emerged below them on the lawn. He called something to Killy and caught the football when his grandson threw it to him.

Noah made a rough sound and reached for the

glass. His eyes met Gage's. He smiled mockingly and lifted it.

The instinct to stop him was automatic. Immediate. "Noah—"

"You expect me to fail, Gage." Noah swirled the glass. "Every single time. You expect it." He turned the glass over and poured the shot harmlessly over the railing. Then he turned the glass upside down and thumped it on the table between them. "I'm not drinking it because you've stopped me. I'm just not drinking so I can prove you wrong."

Then he, too, disappeared inside.

The next morning, Rory knew that Gage was gone.

He didn't show up at the barn to load the spreader.

He wasn't in the office with her dad when she showed up there after mucking the stalls on her own.

He wasn't in the kitchen with Bart.

And the low-slung black car that had been parked for so many weeks now outside the Brown cabin was gone.

She told herself that was fine. That was good. That he could dream on if he thought she would chase after him.

She spent the morning settling bills with departing guests, confirming more reservations for the coming weekend and ordering Christmas gifts online for Killy now that she'd gotten a peek at the letter he'd written to Santa.

The only thing that jarred her carefully modulated equilibrium was discovering that Noah was still there.

She discovered that particular fact when she returned to the lodge with Killy after picking him up from the bus stop. Noah was in the storeroom with Bart, unloading a supply of canned goods, and she stopped cold at the sight of him.

Mostly because at first glance she'd thought he was Gage.

Not that she would ever admit it.

She sent Killy on ahead. "Go and see Grandpa in the office," she told him, and because it was their usual routine, he saw nothing unusual in it at all.

After he was gone, she dangled his backpack from her fingertips. "You're here," she finally said to Noah.

He was still standing there with a giant can of tomatoes in each hand, and his expression was wary. "Is that okay?"

"Gage isn't." Just saying his name made the hollow feeling inside her worsen.

"No."

She wasn't going to ask if he would return. Or where he'd gone. She'd always known his stay at Angel River would come to an end. Now it had.

"Come to the office when you're finished with Bart," she said, heading through the doorway into the kitchen. "You can fill out the paperwork."

"For what?"

She didn't stop. "To get on the payroll." She ignored Bart's raised eyebrows as she walked past him.

In the great room, she threw away a crumpled napkin and stuck a stray glass in the rack of dishes waiting to be washed behind the mahogany bar.

She continued out of the great room and soon heard Killy chattering about his day to her father.

She let the sound of his voice wash over her. She drew in a deep breath and went into the office. Her dad was seated behind the desk.

"Killy," Sean interrupted him. "Bart has a whole batch of Christmas cookies that I think he needs your help with decorating."

Her son dashed past her and disappeared down the hall.

She sat down and began pulling stuff from his backpack in search of his usual worksheets. She pulled out another dinosaur; she wasn't even sure where he'd gotten it. The worksheets were crumpled at the bottom, and she tugged them out, smoothing them on the coffee table.

"I'm selling Angel River," her dad said.

She blinked, certain she hadn't heard right. "What?"

"I'm selling Angel River."

She shot off the couch. Panic filled her. "But why? You can't! Angel River's our home. It means... means everything to you."

"It does," he said quietly.

She whirled around to face him again, fresh alarm making her voice catch. "Is your cancer back?"

He sighed. "No."

"Then...then why?" Tears burned behind her eyes. "Everything's g-getting better." She spread her arms. "Angel River's even a trending topic!"

"I've had an offer for a while," he said. "A long while. And I think it's time I took it. You need to go, Rory."

"What?" She laughed brokenly. Disbelievingly. "You're kicking me out?"

"I'm telling you that it's time for you to start living *your* life."

"This is about Gage, isn't it?" She swiped her nose. "He's the one who talked you into selling."

"He didn't talk me into anything. But in a way, this *is* about him. He asked you to go with him."

She gaped. "He told you?"

"And you picked a fight because it was safer than taking another chance."

It stung harshly because in her heart, she knew it was true. "How can I want to be with a man who doesn't know what family means? He has a grandmother who doesn't even know he exists! Family should never be ignored like that!"

Her father's eyebrows lifted. "The way you've ignored the fact that Killian has a father he's never met?"

"Jon was the one who left us. Why should I give him another opportunity to reject Killian?"

"He hurt you. I'm no fan of the guy. But regardless of Jon's failures, Killian deserves to at least meet the man. Maybe Jon won't care. But then it'll truly be his failing. Not yours. And Killian will survive because he is surrounded by people who love him no matter what." He stood and rounded the desk, catching her chin in his hand. "You are in love with Gage Stanton. Am I wrong?"

When he looked at her that way, she could no more lie now than she could when she'd been a girl. "No."

"Then what the hell are you doing here, Rory?"

"You can't sell Angel River," she whispered.

"I can and I will if you don't get your butt in gear and go after that man," he said with as much vigor as he had in days long past. "And don't worry about Killian. I got you to school when you were his age. I can still do it now."

"B-but…right *now*?"

"You think the world is going to wait on you?"

She wiped the tears from her cheeks. "I don't even know where to find him."

Her dad just gave her a look. "I do."

Rory stared at the tall skyscraper and felt her nerves flagging.

She'd driven half the night to get there. Now it was morning. The street behind her was teeming with buses and cars and pedestrians walking with their heads lowered against the snowflakes swirling around them. Which fit in with the big snow-flake decorations affixed to the light posts lining the street.

Gage didn't merely live in the behemoth towering in front of her. Stanton Development was head-quartered there. And Gage owned all of it.

And she felt wholly unequipped to deal with this Gage Stanton.

She needed the one who'd muck out a horse stall and set up a simple fish aquarium.

The doorman was still holding the door for her, waiting patiently despite the weather.

She shook her head at him in silent apology and backed away, nearly bumping into the woman behind her. She veered around her. She'd go home. She'd figure out a way to keep her dad from selling Angel River.

Except he'd been pretty plain.

"Rory?" An overly cheery voice followed her. "Is that you?"

Rory turned and knew she was losing her marbles for sure. "Willow?"

The other woman giggled. "I *knew* that was you. What are you doing here? You came to see Gage?" Before Rory could stop her, she'd slipped her arm through Rory's and was pulling her out of the snow, right past the patient doorman and into the lobby dominated by an enormous Christmas tree. She flashed some sort of badge as they passed a security desk and hit an elevator button while Rory was still trying to figure out what Tig's flavor of the month was doing at Stanton Tower.

"What are *you* doing here?"

"Didn't Gage tell you?" Willow giggled again and pulled her into the elevator car. "I work here."

Rory's stomach swooped with the bullet-fast ascent. "Since when?"

"Since last month." Willow shrugged her shoulders, slipping out of her coat. She wore a plain brown jacket and trousers, looking nothing like she had when she'd been at the ranch. "Tig and I broke up. He's married, you know."

"I know," Rory said faintly. "But why here?"

"Gage told me if I ever needed a job to call his office. And I did." She smiled brilliantly. "I'm just a receptionist, but a girl has to start somewhere, right?"

Rory's stomach swooped again when the elevator suddenly slowed and eased to a stop. The doors opened smoothly and Willow stepped out. Rory mindlessly followed, her overwhelmed senses barely taking in the sleek industrial decor and the same holiday music that had been piped into the elevator. They passed endless windows and Willow entered another doorway. "Did he offer you a job, too?"

Rory looked away from the massive aquarium wall where brilliantly colored fish as big as her arm darted through the water to yet another Christmas tree with brightly wrapped gifts crammed beneath it. She laughed brokenly. "Honestly, Willow, I don't know what he offered me."

"What did you want me to offer?"

She spun and stared mutely up at Gage.

His jaw was smooth, his espresso hair brushed ruthlessly back from his handsome face. He wore a dark gray suit and tie and a watch that probably cost as much as her pickup truck. Her mouth was dry, and every doubt that had plagued her on the long drive there clamored inside her, just aching to escape. "I... Hi."

With a serious expression on his face, he took her elbow and drew her into an office with a wall of windows and closed the door.

She moistened her lips as she noticed the expansive desk and the rest of the expensive furnishings. The bottom floor of her cabin could have fit inside this office. "I don't know what I'm doing here," she whispered. She nervously walked across the office toward the windows. Snowflakes fell against the glass and slid downward, collecting in slight little drifts at the bottom before even they tumbled out of sight.

It was dizzying.

She turned back around and looked at Gage. He'd moved to lean against his desk, his eyes watchful.

"I shouldn't have said what I did about you and your grandmother." Her jaw worked. "My father pointed that out to me."

His eyes narrowed slightly. And still he said nothing.

She tugged on her ponytail. She felt underdressed in her jeans and red coat and wished she'd taken the time to dress with more care. "I told Noah we were putting him on the payroll." She smiled weakly. "Don't know if that'll last once you've purchased the ranch but—"

"I'm not buying Angel River. I told you that."

"But my dad has an offer. He told me."

"Yeah. From Tig."

She jerked.

"He told me about it when we first got to Angel River. Tig's wanted to buy the place for nearly a year. Every time he visits, he ups the ante." Gage's expression was unreadable. "Might as well know I kept that from you, too."

She winced.

"What did you want me to offer, Rory?"

She tugged at the buttons on her coat. Rocked on her heels. "Everything," she said huskily.

"What if everything I have isn't good enough?"

Her eyes flew to his.

"I don't know how to be anything other than what I am." His voice was low. "Some things I do pretty well." His gaze roved over the office. "And some things—" He looked at her. "The most important things, I've messed up every single time."

And just that easily, she recognized the man he was. The one who made her a bed of flowers. Whose touch made her feel whole. It didn't matter if he had manure on his boots or an expensive watch on his wrist. It was the man inside—the brother who kept trying, the man who kept learning, the one she'd laughed with and cried with. That was the man he was.

The man she was terrified of losing.

"I love you. You didn't mess up *us*. I did that. Because you were right. I was afraid. Afraid of finding everything that I've ever wanted in you and… and losing it."

"Do you think you're alone in that?" His eyes met hers, and she saw in them all her own fears reflecting back at her.

She was quaking inside. "Do you love me?"

His brows drew together. "I asked you to come with me, Rory. You and Killy. I want *you* for my family. I don't say that to other people. I say that to you. If that's not love, I don't know what it is."

She blinked back her tears. "Then is the offer still open?"

His expression softened. "Nothing's changed in the last day, sweetheart, except we're not in your territory. We're in mine."

She took a step closer. Then another. Until she was running into his arms and she could feel his heart hammering just as unevenly as her own. "I don't care about everything you have." She stared into his eyes. "Because everything you are is exactly good enough."

He touched her cheek and she felt the fine tremble in his fingers. "Are you sure?"

She didn't know what exactly the future would hold. But she knew she only wanted it to be with him.

She covered his fingers with her own. "Positive. I just have one question, though."

"What's that?"

"Are we spending Christmas at your place or mine? Because Killy's going to want to tell Santa where we'll be."

Gage's smile was suddenly wide and brilliant. "I think we can figure that one out together."

Together.

She'd never realized before what a beautiful word it was.

* * * * *

Don't miss
the next installment of
New York Times *bestselling author*
Allison Leigh's
Return to the Double C series
Available August 2021
exclusively from
Harlequin Special Edition.

#2803 A COWBOY'S CHRISTMAS CAROL

Montana Mavericks: What Happened to Beatrix?
by Brenda Harlen

Evan Cruise is haunted by his past and refuses to celebrate the festivities around him—until he meets Daphne Taylor. But when Daphne uncovers Evan's shocking family secret, it threatens to tear them apart. Will a little Christmas magic change everything?

#2804 A TEMPORARY CHRISTMAS ARRANGEMENT

The Bravos of Valentine Bay • by Christine Rimmer

Neither Harper Bravo nor Lincoln Stryker is planning to stay in Valentine Bay. But when Lincoln moves in next door and needs a hand with his nice and nephew, cash-strapped Harper can't help but step in. They make a deal: just during the holiday season, she'll nanny the kids while he works. But will love be enough to have them both changing their plans?

#2805 HIS LAST-CHANCE CHRISTMAS FAMILY

Welcome to Starlight • by Michelle Major

Brynn Hale has finally returned home to Starlight. She's ready for a fresh start for her son, and what better time for it than Christmas? Still, Nick Dunlap is the one connection to her past she can't let go of. Nick's not sure he deserves a chance with her now, but the magic of the season might make forgiveness—and love—a little bit easier for them both...

#2806 FOR THIS CHRISTMAS ONLY

Masterson, Texas • by Caro Carson

A chance encounter at the town's Yule log lighting leads Eli Taylor to invite Mallory Ames to stay with him. Which turns into asking her to be his fake girlfriend to show his siblings what a genuinely loving partnership looks like...just while they visit for the holidays. But will their lesson turn into something real for both of them?

#2807 A FIREHOUSE CHRISTMAS BABY

Lovestruck, Vermont • by Teri Wilson

After her dreams of motherhood were dashed, Felicity Hart is determined to make a fresh start in Lovestruck. Unfortunately, she has to work with firefighter Wade Ericson when a baby is abandoned at the firehouse. Then Felicity finds herself moving into Wade's house and using her foster-care training to care for the child, all just in time for Christmas.

#2808 A SOLDIER UNDER HER TREE

Sweet Briar Sweethearts • by Kathy Douglass

When her ex-fiancé shows up at her shop—engaged to her sister!—dress designer Hannah Carpenter doesn't know what to do. Especially when former fling Russell Danielson rides to the rescue, offering a fake relationship to foil her rude relations. The thing is, there's nothing fake about his kiss...

---

*Brynn Hale, single mom widowed after an unhappy
marriage, has finally returned home to Starlight.
She's ready for a fresh start for her son, and what
better time for it than Christmas? But Nick Dunlap is
the one connection to her past she can't let go of...*

*Read on for a sneak peek at the next book in the
Welcome to Starlight miniseries,*
His Last-Chance Christmas Family
by Michelle Major.

"You sound like a counselor." The barest glimmer of
a smile played around the edges of Brynn's mouth.
"When did you get so smart, Chief Dunlap?"

"I was born this way. You never noticed before now
because you were too dazzled by my good looks."

Her eyes went wide for a moment, and he wondered
if he'd overstepped with the teasing. "I was dazzled
by you. That part is true." She rolled her eyes. "But I
guarantee you didn't show this kind of insight when we
were younger."

He should make some funny comment back to her,
keep the moment light. Instead, he let his gaze lower to
her mouth as he took the soft ends of her hair between

his fingers. "I might not have messed things up so badly if I had."

She drew in a sharp breath and he stepped away. This was not the time to spook her. "Come on, Brynn," he coaxed. "We both know it's not going to be good for anyone if you stay with your mom."

"She doesn't even want to meet Remi," Brynn told him, her full lips pressing into a thin line.

"Her loss," he said quietly. "All along it's been her loss. Say yes. Please."

She shifted and looked to where Tyler had disappeared with Kel. Without turning back to Nick, she nodded. "Yes," she said finally. "Thank you for the offer. I appreciate it and promise we won't disrupt your life." Now she did turn to him. "Very much, anyway," she added with a smile.

"Easy as pie," he said, ignoring the fact that his heart was beating as fast as if he'd just finished running a marathon.

Don't miss
His Last-Chance Christmas Family *by Michelle Major,*
available December 2020 wherever
Harlequin Special Edition books and ebooks are sold.

Harlequin.com